The Paper Wife

THE PAPER WIFE

Linda Spalding

THE ECCO PRESS

THE ECCO PRESS

100 West Broad Street

Hopewell, New Jersey 08525

Printed in the United States of America

Library of Congress Cataloging-in-Publication Data

Spalding, Linda

The paper wife / Linda Spalding

p.   cm.

ISBN 0-88001-453-9 (case)

ISBN 0-88001-524-1 (paperback)

I. Title.

PS3569.P3386P36   1996

813'.54—dc20   95-26729

9   8   7   6   5   4   3   2   1

FIRST PAPERBACK EDITION 1997

I want to thank first, Michael, for help from the beginning to the end. I thank my mother, Edith Dickinson, for belief; my daughters, Esta and Kristin, for counsel; Connie and Leon Rooke for reading and advice; Martha Butterfield for The Last Things; Harry Mroz for technology. I heartily thank my editors, Louise Dennys at Knopf Canada and Liz Calder at Bloomsbury for friendship and tenacity; and Susan Burns for considering everything. Also, the Canada Council and the Ontario Arts Council for generous grants. The Villa Serbelloni. And Chiapas.

...here your sisters, broken
into women, entering another stranger's dream

Deborah Digges

In memory of my brother,
Skip Dickinson

One

I CROSSED THE BORDER AT ElPaso. I was running away. As if that could make things right. I paid for my ticket and climbed aboard a bus with statues on the dashboard and a crucifix dangling from the mirror. Mary was up there too, with her baby in her arms.

The driver looked at me as if he knew everything. And an old man sitting next to the only empty seat stared at me hard, his legs jutting out in the aisle. I could see him from the steps. He was huge, sitting with a sack of fruit between his feet, but I squeezed down the aisle with my suitcase. I said, "Excuse me. Excuse me," and the old man moved his cane but not his legs, so that I had to crawl over him, trying not to feel his knees against the back of mine and trying not to step on the sack of fruit.

I was surrounded by flesh. The shoulder of the old man rubbed against me and there were people jammed into seats and standing in the aisle, children crying, even animals. I stared out the window, looking back at what I'd left behind. Everything. The bus picked up speed. Of course, Kate wouldn't be stopped by the thought of a border. I'd left her a note explaining what I could, but that wasn't much. I told her I was going to Mexico. I said I needed time by myself. But we'd made a vow years before that nothing — nobody — would ever come between us. Not family or friend or job. And not boy. Or man.

I pressed my face against the window and closed my eyes. There were smells outside and inside, the smells of fumes held under the earth, under the skin. We stopped at a small shack on the highway and took on more passengers. Crates full of chickens were tied on the roof. The center of gravity changed. Now the bus rocked back and forth on the road like a pendulum.

The old man next to me held out an orange, one of the ones he'd brought in the transparent sack at his feet. I took it and turned it over in my hand. Good. Fuel that was taking me away. I'll do what ever I have to do and get it over with, I thought. The old man fell asleep. His mouth fell open and he clutched his cane.

I'd bought a sandwich in El Paso, where it was safe to buy food. Now I tried to unwrap it quietly. The old man was fat enough. Then I stopped to stare out the window. God's children — that's what my grandmother would have said. Perhaps I should share what I had. The landscape pulled past and past, mescal and other cactus, melting adobe brick and sky. It was not like any place I'd ever seen. There was fringe across the front window by the saints, and outside on the fenders there were vases of flowers. The crucifix swung back and forth. The driver had crossed himself when we started, but now he was talking to the man behind him as if he were not in charge of my life. He used the same voice my grandmother used when she was talking to God.

When I was seven, I went to live with her, after my mother died. But I spent the first part of my childhood on the

Kansas prairie, in a house by a creek. And railroad tracks — they went right past our door. I remember my mother looking out with one hand above her eyes to shade them. There was the fender shop, the grocery store, the post office, and the school. Two churches, the Methodist one and the Christian one. The fields. They lay under the sky. There were cows to be milked and cows to be butchered and eaten.

Then my mother died in an accident and my father took me to my grandmother's to live. We spent a long time, a day and night, on the train and then we alighted, stepping out like acrobats. The house was at the bottom of Colorado and it was nothing but a door standing up against the sky and underneath it a room where my grandmother lived. I remember opening that door and going down the stairs, my father holding me by the collar of my blouse. My grandfather had dug the basement before he died but he'd never put a house on top. There were tiny windows in the walls at ground level and a flat, tarpaper roof. "I brought her," my father said, but I didn't know if he meant me or my mother. It seemed he was going to bury both of us.

My grandmother made her living sewing for the church, and her skin was like one of the bolts of cloth she turned into altar coverings. For a minute we stood in the dark, listening to a kettle boil. Father and child. The place was overpowering in its difference from us, and I wanted to lie down. I wanted to curl up on the bed I could see in the corner but I stood still and asked for a glass of milk. "Please," I said, because I didn't want her to think my parents hadn't raised me right.

My father looked relieved. "That's the first word out of her in two days," he said.

"I've made up a bed," my grandmother told him. "It's behind the curtain, next to mine." Her underground house had four rooms created between fabric walls.

Later a truck drove up with the wooden box that had been behind us in the baggage car. "I'll put her where you want," my father said, as if my grandmother might have made up a bed for my mother too. I stood on tiptoes and looked out one of the windows while my father and the truck driver dug a big hole. Then I watched them put my mother in. "She'll be right on the other side of the wall," my grandmother said.

My father came back in and washed his hands and stood in the doorway holding a cup of coffee and his hat. "Well now, Biff," my grandmother said to him calmly, for nobody in that county denied a person liquid on a summer day, "you drink up. Lily Ann has things to do around here." Then she looked at him darkly. "And she's all I have left."

"I guess," he said, tucking his chin into his collar uneasily and swallowing the scalding drink. I didn't think it was the last time he would stand there squinting against the darkness, but that's what it was. It was the last time he would watch my grandmother walk to the tiny windows to pull down the shades — my grandmother, the mother of his dead wife. It was like water, that room, with the green material pulled down against the light. And my grandmother's tall, thin body was poised in its figured dress, its rolled-down stockings and black shoes. My father's face had a film of perspiration on it, and the back of his shirt was damp.

"See your father to the door, Lily Ann," my grandmother said.

Easter shoes, patent leather, that's what I had on, and

they were still so new they creaked when I crossed the floor. Then my hand was reaching for the knob and in a minute I saw him disappear.

Alongside the tracks there were poles all the way back to the house where I'd lived with my mother and father, and on the train I'd been saying those words in my mind as the poles went by. Mother and father, mother and father. I hadn't said the words out loud. I knew the poles were just poles, nothing else, with wires hanging down and billboards underneath. Burma Shave. Quaker Oats. I didn't live in that house any more. I'd been taken by my father's hand to live with Zozzie, my grandmother, where I learned my new life. I was an outsider.

It was summer and it got hotter every day until my grandmother's house began to crack. The roof hissed and the pipes dried up. Our beds were pools of heat and I was so heavy that I dreamed. The house in flames but always underwater, like the truck that was lying at the bottom of the creek. Or sometimes I dreamed that I'd died like my mother, that I was a ghost who'd stepped out of the truck without bones. Then I'd push my face against the wall of Zozzie's house. It had a shiny yellow surface. Nobody knew me in her town. They remembered my mother, of course, but what did they know about me?

That summer was hotter than anything before or since. The numbers involved in the temperature were said like an incantation for days in a row, over the radio and by anyone on the street. My grandmother sat in front of an electric fan which blew air over an old dishpan she had once bathed my mother in. The darkness around us was unrelieved by anything except a shaded lamp and the small windows at the top of the wall and the hooded lights over her violets. There were violets everywhere, living under electric bulbs. Zozzie sat on a wicker chair and I sat with her in the dark, because I had no choice. We listened to the news and the farm reports and to nothing and I drew pictures while my grandmother sat, stiff and shattered, in front of the fan, holding straight pins in her long, straight mouth. Once or twice I started a letter to my father, but what could I say? He lived on without me. He'd never wanted me to stay.

Zozzie didn't just sew for the local churches. She took orders from other towns in other states. She made altar cloths and robes and shawls and the small embroidered pieces that are draped over babies before baptism. Chrisoms, they're called. All this she did among the violets between the cloth partitions of her underground cave.

"Is Daddy coming soon?" I'd ask. "Did he write to you about me?"

Zozzie only coughed and sat back in her chair, although her body didn't fit it very well, she was so tall. She'd push the afghan off her knees to show me a length of silk full of feathery stitches and french knots. "Look. Blue for love. Red for life. Every picture and color means something."

"Why?"

"It's a different way to tell a story. The sword here guards the gates to paradise." She pointed. "Over here, these grapes growing on a vine mean the Promised Land."

"What's that?"

"The place everybody's looking for."

"Mama — is she there or is she outside in the yard?"

My grandmother stood up and the colors fell off her lap. "Your mama ran away," she said. "But she didn't get very far. She's right here with us."

The next day we tried to re-enact one of the picnics that had been part of my mother's childhood. I helped boil the eggs and make the sandwiches. The ancient basket with its moldy top was washed. We didn't use mayonnaise because my grandmother had seen five Christians die after eating potato salad shortly before she was married. And we didn't say grace because we had little to be thankful for. That first summer it seemed that any grace held the threat of remembering too much. Later my grandmother would talk to God again, but for a while that year she said it required too much volume. We carried the picnic basket to the front room and sat on the floor. We didn't go outside because my grandmother didn't like the sun. We ate in the humid kitchen underground. Then we washed the dishes, rinsed them with boiling water from the kettle, and dried them with one of the tea towels she had hemmed.

In town people relied on secrets, Zozzie said. Secrets and lies. But we relied on each other. We'd tell each other everything. She listened to farm reports and religious programs turned up on the radio. She loved the intricate and morbidly descriptive weather forecasts. Tornadoes were something she believed in. She believed in wrath. She sealed the windows and the door against predators. "After school, I want you to get on the bus and come straight home," she warned.

But by September, when school started, I couldn't always do that. I knew what I wanted. I'd been following Kate Hampshire all over town.

When Kate went to the dime store with her mother to buy her tablets and pencils, I was behind her in the check-out line. I watched her trying on saddle shoes at Jensons and I saw her buy socks and underwear and a new skirt and blouse. I knew what size she wore and what colors she liked. I knew what her mother approved of in the way of clothing and where they went for butterscotch sodas after they shopped.

When I found Kate we were eight years old, and she'd never been outside of her own yard alone except when she walked to school along the sidewalk the way she was supposed to. She belonged to a family and a house standing among the white birch trees her father had planted, but I talked to her for the first time on the school playground one recess when she was picking out her softball team. She had long, dark hair and bruises on both knees and she was wearing the saddle shoes I'd watched her trying on. When the bell rang, she strolled over and stood in front of me. "Do you even know how to play?" she demanded, leaning over to scrape the packed dirt off those new shoes with a stick. I shook my head but I followed her to the glass doors of the school, which was full of yellow wood and linoleum. "Where'd you come here from, anyway?" she said.

At first I told her the truth. Then she said, "My dad was a spy in the war. What was yours?"

"He's in Korea," I lied. "Fighting. He's an officer. But my mother's actually dead."

Kate looked convinced. "I know," she said. "That's too bad."

That day after school, I followed her home. I found out where she lived, even though she hadn't picked me for her team. I saw the white house, the trees, the pattern the leaves made on the grass, and from that day forward they were joined together in my mind — the perfect symmetry of the Hampshire house and the tall, perfect daughter. A path led up to the door. The shallow steps were carefully cemented.

Later, out on the playground by myself, I struck a ball clear across it into the field behind the orphanage next to our school. My mother was dead. My father was gone for good. That ball was for Kate. I would just wait until she invited me in.

The orphanage was tall and old, made of red brick and separated from our playground by a high, chain-link fence. Sometimes I watched the orphans when they came outside, but most of the time I kept my eyes on Kate. I used to stand outside her house at night on the lawn her parents had created, although nobody else had lawns yet in that town, they had back yards and front yards. The Hampshires had hired a Mexican gardener and transformed their back yard into a place with its own grove of birch trees, from which, a few years later, I cut bracelets for their daughter, although she would not have dared to cut the thin skin of those trees herself. I suppose the black bands I left on the trunks are still there, if the trees, the lawn, if anything is there, but that fall I stood between the peony beds and the birch trees at the far end of the lawn many times and wished the Hampshires would adopt me. I'd give up my father's name and be their second, perfect daughter.

At night the curtains were drawn at the Hampshires', but they were drawn carelessly and I could see the three of them through the parting of material sitting in their matching chairs watching TV, their clothes arranged stiffly around them as if they weren't part of the natural world. The house around them was like that too. It was perfect. Mr. Hampshire napped in a corner. He was a lawyer, I had found that out, and sometimes Kate and Mrs. Hampshire would look at each other in the way that women do when they're putting up with a man. Mrs. Hampshire made things out of tin, using huge shears — at least, that's what she was doing while I stood outside in their yard that year. For several months she worked on a large, intricate wreath for the front door, while Kate watched the TV set and dressed and undressed her dolls. For months I climbed out of my grandmother's house and walked up the highway to the Hampshires' neighborhood to push through the thick box hedge and stand in the perfume of the spicebush and the shadow of the crab-apple tree and look through their windows because Kate was inside on the other side of the glass.

When I was finally invited in, Kate took me upstairs to her room and it was everything I had imagined. She had bookcases and a row of dolls on a window-seat and a dressing table with curtained arms that opened to reveal drawers. The drawers were full of plastic barrettes that looked like French poodles or colored bows, and handkerchiefs with ballet dancers twirling in the corners, and bath powders and small bottles of make-believe cologne. The dolls had names. She got a new one every year under the Christmas tree. Each of them had its own clothes. "I love each one best for a year," Kate told me.

"Is that the way you are with everyone?"

"I don't love real people. They're not the same."

"Not even your parents?"

"Well, but that's not the kind of love you decide on, is it? When I decide on somebody, it'll be for good."

She showed me her mother's dressing room, where each thing lay in its own beautiful tray or container. There was a silk-covered box with small slots for stockings — her mother bought them at Jensons but she unwrapped them as soon as she brought them home and washed them in vinegar. Everything in the Hampshire house was washed after purchase. The underwear was ironed and the hairbrushes were soaked and then dried in the sun. Soap was hardened in linen closets. Sheets were turned so they didn't wear out. Blankets were aired. Furniture and floors were polished until they shone like mirrors.

On Saturdays Kate and I were sent outside while the vacuum cleaner made noise all day and Mrs. Flores, the maid, went up and down the stairs with a bucket and rags. On rainy days we played in the attic, where there were racks of evening clothes and clothes for another season wrapped up in plastic, and where the roof made a peak overhead. We were forbidden to touch the walls because the insulation that poked through had filaments of glass in it, like the angel hair Mrs. Hampshire used to decorate the house at Christmas time. There was a small window in the peak of the roof, though, and after the sun set we used to climb up the wall and lie with our bellies against the insulation, looking out. We could see everything from up there. "Pull your shirt down or your stomach will get red. And don't you dare tell on me," Kate would say. But she knew I wouldn't. She already trusted me completely.

It never occurred to me to ask her back to my grandmother's to play. What had been mine was gone. I couldn't claim the underground house with its cloth partitions separating the four rooms where we lived. In one corner were the beds, in another corner a table, a sink, a stove. At the front, where the stairs came down from outside, there was the wicker furniture. And finally a corner for the bath.

I'd been waiting to hear from my father, but no letter came. For Christmas he sent me a silver dollar, and I put it away in the drawer by my bed. And although I didn't miss him in particular, I remember missing the warm fur of the dog who'd run away, the clotted fur I used to dig my hands into. Underneath the white fur there had been a shorter, lighter layer. Then there was the invisible skin.

My grandmother and I went on living side by side. There was the radio in the morning during breakfast, and the sound of the sewing machine, the frying pan, the kettle, the pipes overhead stretching and opening. Sometimes the roof sounded like gunfire. But I grew accustomed to those sounds. It seemed possible, as my grandmother said, that people from town were walking over us and whispering things. "Try not to listen," she said, pulling her needle through a long strip of cloth. Red for life. Blue for love. White for innocence.

My grandmother's desk was full of stationery, as if she might sit there to write a letter any time, although there was no one for her to write to any more and the paper had my grandfather's business letterhead on every page. Along with the useless stationery, his thick, white business cards were wedged in a little box next to the ink bottles and blotters. In fact, the desk was full of him. His smell lived on in the drawer and I pulled it out and sniffed at it, trying to know him. At the back I found three letters to my mother folded and tucked like nestlings. They were from my father, but someone had put them there, hidden away.

I remember that my father's handwriting was terrible, and there weren't many words because someone had taken scissors to these pieces of paper, crudely chopping out some of the passages. As I read and reread, it seemed to me that the words cut out were the crucial ones, and I began to think of my father as a man who had once been desperate enough to write things that alarmed or excited my mother. Had she mutilated these letters and then hidden them away, or had my grandmother done this damage to him?

I could imagine my father at the other end of this communication, lying on a small iron bed, the same one he and my mother slept in later on. He lay on the same bed by the same creek in Everest on land owned by someone else. I knew the bed, the bedside lamp, even the man who owned the land. His name was Mr. Malcolm and everybody loved him, that's what my mama had said. On the base of the lamp was a lady holding a lute. Of course the lute wasn't real; it didn't play; but that didn't matter to us.

I imagined my father sitting up slowly, pulling his suspenders up over his arms. He'd been working outside all day and he was tired, so he sat dangling his legs over the edge of the bed and holding the letter out under the light to make it easier to see. He had the letter in his hand, but he seemed to be defeated by its weight. He sat bent over himself on the edge of the iron bed, wearied by the simple task of writing it. Already, my mother was difficult to please.

"Zozzie? Who was Mama with? When she had the accident?"

"His name was Mr. Malcolm. He owned your farm."

It was the fact that she had included me in this secret that intrigued me more than the news itself. I knew my mother had died in Mr. Malcolm's truck. Perhaps I already knew what that meant. But no one had told me about it; I'd had to figure it out for myself. In a small town there are stories everywhere. Every patch of land has its story and the living mingle with the dead. Truth is like silverware, hidden in closets or under beds. Nobody takes it out. I never took Kate to my grandmother's house in all the years I was her closest friend. I made up a false address. I told her I lived in a farmhouse that had a pointed roof and a real front porch. And, strangely, Kate never asked for evidence. She told people at school that my grandmother didn't like intruders, which was accurate enough. She became my apologist. And I became like one of her dolls. Chosen. Better than a blood relative.

With her fingers Zozzie made a bee that buzzed at my stomach or a bird that snapped at my nose, but otherwise she didn't touch me. She didn't lift me when I fell. She said she was too old for that. After I arrived she took all her church orders over the phone and I delivered her work to the post office when it was done. She used the phone to order whatever we needed to survive. It didn't amount to much. We ate grilled cheese sandwiches and a bowl of soup most nights. She made all my clothes. I picked up the bread and cheese and soup and cloth when I was in town. In town, I was Zozzie's ears and eyes.

On Sundays I ate dinner at the Hampshires' and, when I

was lucky, even though it was a school night, I was allowed to stay overnight. Sometimes I forgot to bring my clothes so Kate would let me wear something of hers. Then it wasn't so hard to walk like Kate and talk like Kate. I studied her carefully. I already resembled her; people said we looked like sisters. It was the coloring, the height, the nose and mouth. Now, while we sat around our TV trays eating TV dinners in front of Perry Mason, I practiced her delicate hold on the knife and fork, leaning back between mouthfuls, as if I had all the time in the world to experience the pleasures it offered me.

For some reason, my grandmother did not object to any of this. She approved of the Hampshires for reasons of her own. Kate's grandfather had helped my grandfather negotiate the purchase of the piece of land into which he had dug the hole lined with cement where Zozzie lived. The underground rooms with the radio and the desk with pictures and cards underneath a piece of glass. The yellow walls with their stains and marks. The painted beds.

After school Kate went to ballet lessons or piano lessons and I took a bus home. I went home with a paper sack full of groceries in one arm and my books in the other. I sat on the bus alone, at the back, where nobody would be likely to notice me.

It was different with Kate. Eventually she even took me to the country club, although these visits were parceled out carefully because members were only allowed to bring the same guest once a month. Then one night she asked her mother why they couldn't use other names for me so I could come more often. Unfortunately, her father overheard this conversation. "Suppose someone were to lie to me? How could I represent him?" he said indignantly. "Truth is essential to civilization. Let's keep that in mind while we go in and enjoy our dinner."

Kate said, "Daddy, I've never brought anyone here except Lily, so what difference does it make? If it's Lily or somebody else, what's the difference?" We had just driven into the parking lot of the club. It was a summer night and there were people getting out of cars in fresh, ironed dresses and seersucker suits and polished shoes. A boy and girl sat in a dark convertible under the clubhouse lights. I was entering this paradise again with the Hampshires after a full day of swimming at the club pool with Kate. We'd already learned that I could eat dinner on the days I swam there without signing the register again. Guests got their hands stamped and the small black star was good for a day. The ink was so indelible that it didn't come off in the pool, but the stamp might be something else on the following day. A chicken. A tree. A half-moon. "It's the intent of a law that matters," Kate said quietly.

"That's all very well," Mr. Hampshire said, opening the car door for us, "but as long as there are rules, you'll abide by them, young lady." We got out of the car — two grownups, two children — although Kate and I were not really children any more.

"But some rules aren't reasonable," Kate pointed out. "And sometimes we think rules are sacred when they aren't. Remember that man who didn't stop for the police?"

Mr. Hampshire looked down at her. "Why bring that up?"

"It's just how you handled it. Tell Lily. I love that story."

"Well, maybe after we've ordered I'll tell it. If you like." We followed him into the lobby. Everyone ordered a sirloin steak rare, except Mrs. Hampshire, who preferred to have hers medium, and we settled back in our upholstered chairs. "Go on, William," said Mrs. Hampshire, nervously. "Tell them about that man and what you did."

"It's completely beside the point." Mr. Hampshire sounded irritated. Nevertheless he leaned back and reached for the martini which his membership in the club made possible, because in our county, unless you were sitting in a private club, you couldn't buy a mixed drink. "One night this old geezer was leaving a bar, that's all, and one of our boys in blue followed him. Not surprisingly, given the limited nature of their intelligence, they mistook him for a drunk when he was actually a man with a heart condition, driving too cautiously, perhaps. At any rate, they turned the siren on and he didn't stop. He reasoned that he was doing nothing wrong, but they followed him all the way to his house and arrested him."

Kate smiled and nudged me.

"For what?" I asked, to please Kate.

"For failure to stop on command." Mr. Hampshire looked over our heads, as if we weren't there. "But I went back to the books and discovered there was no law about stopping for a siren or a flashing light. None at all."

Mrs. Hampshire picked her napkin up and spread it out on her lap. "But everyone still stops for the police, dear. All the time." We were sitting under a large chandelier and I remembered a night we'd been sitting there, in exactly the same place, when Mr. Hampshire had offered a special dessert to anyone who could guess how many crystals it had. Kate had refused to play. She hated to lose. Now the light lit her skin and hair. Even I, who resembled her in many ways, could see that she was becoming beautiful. "Oh well, as I said, rules are usually there for a reason," Mr.

Hampshire said. Mrs. Hampshire glanced at my hand, which was stamped and poised over the bare white plate in front of me. "That one wasn't on the books, but they got it on the books right away, obviously. We got the old boy off, but that doesn't mean a siren has no place in our society, does it? We might get Lily in here every day if you promise never to bring another friend. We might get the club to accept her, but what happens when the day comes that you'd like to invite someone else?" Mr. Hampshire took a sip of his martini. He kept his liquor in a locker. Each locker had a key. "I'll speak to the manager in your behalf if you consider that and decide to press your suit."

I started to make a joke about pressed suits but I caught the look on Kate's face. "I've decided," she announced flatly, although I couldn't see what his story had to do with our afternoons at the pool, during which we lay in the sun and rubbed baby oil mixed with iodine on each other and talked about torture and boys. We felt slightly guilty about our afternoons in the bright heat. We thought they were dangerous and abnormal. We didn't mention this to each other because we didn't have to. "Only Lily will come here with me," Kate said. We knew the heavy thud of the diving boards as they were released by a body springing upwards. Then the splash. Without looking we knew whether the diver was a boy or a girl. Even the spring of the board was a signal, and the lifeguard's fierce whistle was a mark in the time that went on for ever. The shouting, pushing children who were not allowed to run. The smell of lassitude and energy thrown together, the sleepy mothers in scarves and curlers sitting on towels.

There were two country clubs in town, and the Hampshires belonged to this one because it had a tennis court and accepted Jews. Mr. Hampshire had played tennis in college. He wasn't Jewish but he wouldn't join a club from which Jews were excluded. Of course, a club is a private organization and can make whatever rules it wishes; it isn't governed by the U.S. Constitution, as he was the first to admit. But there was the matter of personal principles.

Mr. Hampshire had been a lieutenant in the navy during the war, working in Air Combat Intelligence. He referred to himself as a former ACI officer. "Figure it out," Kate would say. "Intelligence. That means spying. That's what he did." It was hard to tell how she felt about this, or rather, her feelings seemed to change over the years, just as they did about the country club and her father's political power and the privileges her family enjoyed. As we got older, she began to regard privilege as suspect. "Ownership," she shouted once, during an argument with her father. "I hate the whole idea! Owning a tree is just as bad as owning a slave!" She was opposed to the military because it defended property. She wanted to go abroad, to go into the Peace Corps or work for the U.N. But she was part of the reason for the Hampshires' way of life. If it hadn't been for Kate, they would never have joined the country club at all. She liked to swim and it was impossible to use the public pool because of polio. Then there was the matter of the tennis court. Mr. Hampshire was a busy man but he was looking forward to the day when he could take his racket out again.

Kate was the reason for something else. We were in the third grade when Mr. Hampshire realized Kate couldn't spell. Convinced that her inability was due to the abandonment of phonics in the curriculum, he had some business cards printed and ran for election to the local school board. When our schools were desegregated by command of the

U.S. Supreme Court, Mr. Hampshire, still on the school board, had his doubts. "The separate but equal principle has been working in this country since the Emancipation Proclamation," he told us one Sunday night during a break in "Perry Mason". "This entire business is going to upset the community, and there's no reason for it. There's no reason in the world for the federal government to butt into our local affairs. We take care of the colored in this town; we always have. Things that are separate can be equal."

Kate said, "It works in algebra but not in real life, Daddy. It isn't fair to decide things that way." We were in the sixth grade and the legal right to sit under our school's roof had been extended to two girls, Mavis Clark and Clare Bridgeman. Right away, Kate invited them into our scout troop, although when they showed up the scout leader was visibly distressed. "I imagine you girls will want to stay with your own troop," she said to Mavis and Clare. "There's bound to be one in your own neighborhood."

It was true that everyone in the troop lived in Kate's neighborhood except me, and I never went on the overnight trips or the cookouts. "All you need is a bedroll," Kate used to tell me, but there were other things, not so easily defined, that Mavis and Clare and I lacked. Kate told the scout leader she was dropping out unless the two black girls could join. Never mind the privileges of a private club, that wasn't the point, or if it was, she didn't want to belong. She had her father's flair for argument, and her principles were more consistent, therefore easier to defend.

Kate and Mavis had nothing in common that I could see, but they became friends. They sat together at recess, arms linked, sharing private jokes, and I hated Mavis desperately.

That year we were invited to a slumber party, Kate and I, and I agreed to go. It wasn't a girl scout overnight, but there were things I needed to acquire. A better pair of babydoll pajamas. An indoor sleeping bag. I wouldn't have made the effort but it was a chance to go someplace with Kate. Her mother would drop us off, we'd go in the big Lincoln, and in the eyes of the other girls I'd reassert my rights. Suzanne, who was giving the party, was famous for her mother's cookies and the cinnamon rolls she served for breakfast after a night of ghost stories on the basement floor. When we arrived, carrying our things in pillow cases so as not to look too serious, Suzanne met us at the door. "Hi, come on. You guys are late!"

"My mom was on the phone," Kate explained. "Hey, is Mavis coming? You invited her, didn't you?"

"Kate, this is my party, and no, I didn't."

Kate remembered her father's argument about the U.S. Constitution, but she didn't care. "I'm leaving then," she announced quietly. "Come on, Lily, let's go."

Regretting the chocolate chip cookies, I said, "What about Clare? Why don't you make a big deal about her?"

"Oh, for heaven's sake," Kate shot back. "This isn't about color. Mavis is my friend, that's all." She took my hand and we walked all the way back to her house, carrying our pillowcases, mine full of the new pajamas and sleeping bag. I didn't care, after all. I would spend the night at Kate's. She would let me lie close to her in her bed. I would run my hand over her skin under her pajamas and feel the sprouts of hair like a field growing something in the dark. I would be happy. I would be happy. We were almost women. Her skin was like mine. When her breasts grew, they changed the slope of her body, which was angular everywhere else.

And the nipples were large and dark. Her hair was dark and her eyes were brown and opaque, whereas mine told everything. That night, we lay side by side like moths, leaving our dust on the sheets. Our bodies, how secret they were, as if they weren't ready to be claimed.

A year later Kate fell in love with a boy named Andrew Sharp. We had moved up to junior high and Kate went on a hayrack ride with him. From then on she had one crush after another, and I suppose I did too, but mine never amounted to anything real. In high school Kate went out with a boy named Kevin who took her to parties, and sometimes she tried to find someone for me. Sometimes we went on a double date. But in the summer Kate and Kevin went to the drive-in alone and I stayed around the house with Zozzie, peeling vegetables for her to put in jars. "Everybody buys canned food nowadays," I told her crossly. She wanted to teach me all the stitches she knew so that I'd be able to make my own way in the world, but I was too restless to learn. I wanted to be at the Hampshires' watching the Hit Parade or the Kennedy–Nixon debates. Mr. Hampshire said Jack Kennedy was dangerous. "He won't have any commitment to due process, the way he's been raised," he declared from his corner of the living room. But Mrs. Hampshire sat on the couch with Kate and me and said Jack Kennedy looked young and smart. And she liked his wife.

"de Gaulle warned us about getting mired down in that god-forsaken jungle," Mr. Hampshire told his wife one night after the election. "But Jack Kennedy continues to ignore his words, no doubt at our peril." He was sitting on the kitchen stool, having his highball and looking at the paper, and I was lurking in the dining room. "I'm predicting that what's been known through history as honorable disengagement is over and done with. Kaput. For good. After the Cuba mess, young Mr. Kennedy can't afford to look soft. So he's found a place where he can meet the Reds head on and, take my word for it, he won't back down. It's the same war I was fighting twenty years ago but they're going to have to finish it this time."

I was waiting for Kate to come home; we were going to do our homework. It was 1962 and we were taking Spanish. In our town the Mexicans, who came up to work in the mines or for the railroad, sent their children to a different school, because they were Catholic and because they lived in a different part of town, but their extremes of religion and celebration rose up from over there like an intoxication. What was sacred to them was separate from us, almost forbidden. The girls were born wearing earrings — that was how it seemed. We thought they were delicate and cherished. Once, I asked Kate to boil a needle and make holes in my ears, but Mrs. Hampshire found out what we were doing and put a stop to it. She told me I'd look like a Catholic. She didn't like the word "cheap," she said, but Mexican girls were different from us.

"Jack Kennedy's a Catholic," I reminded her.

A year later, when Kennedy was shot, a lot of the girls in our class went straight to Kate's and lay on her bed and cried. The whole country was in mourning. Everything stopped — even traffic. Stores closed. The Kennedys had been perfect. Nothing would ever be the same.

Then one day, after we'd been living for years like unmatched twins, Kate's parents put us in the back seat of their Lincoln and we rolled away from home to enter the new geography of college. We had our bags, boxes, stuffed animals, diaries, and desires. We found the room we would share, and we began our new lives. Our campus was a bright quadrangle of jetting sprinklers surrounded by buildings of sandstone blocks laid one upon another like hands. We were alone together, more or less, at last.

When I think of that first year away from home, what I remember is the smoke-filled, noise-filled front room at Tulagis, a place near campus where we could sit and drink beer in the afternoon or dance and drink beer at night. I remember my table in the library, too, and the sensation I had when I was sitting there conjugating Spanish verbs, I remember everyone sleeping, reading, writing on those heavy tables as if we were bound to them — but I remember eating and drinking and singing around the tables at Tulagis, where we were also bound. Kate and I had known each other more than half our lives. I'd followed her to college, or she'd followed me. We moved in a circle, one after the other, like the hands of a clock that has been overwound.

Outside, the air was as dry and crisp as it had been every autumn afternoon of our lives, but inside, we were different. We were wearing black tights, black turtlenecks, and smoking cigarettes. We'd gone through Rush Week with a mixture of terror and scorn. Kate's mother had given her a black cocktail dress; she'd shown us both how to eat chicken with a knife and fork but I had no black dress, no pearls, no cool grip on the glass. And although there was something about those sororities that appealed to me, as if a door had opened for a moment and revealed a scent, a heavy perfume, Kate saw that I would not be invited to join and she gave up on the idea for herself. Then both of us retreated to Tulagis in the afternoons.

One afternoon in September we were in a booth close to the front window and Kate was telling me about Hugh Pearson, a boy she'd already gone out with several times. "He actually wants me to go to bed with him," she laughed, "and I hardly even know him. So is this going to be the normal course of events?" Over the bar there was a dark painting of dark women, naked, who seemed to represent a future that might be ours, and the windows of the Tule, as we called it, were coated with our breathing and our relief at finding harbor there. Kate's back was against the window but I could see someone behind her, through the glass. I could see him wavering a little on the sidewalk in a corduroy jacket and cowboy boots. The window was covered with pieces of paper — notices stuck there with tape announcing movies and bands — but I could see him standing between announcements and I knew who he was; that morning I'd walked out of class with him. "Where do you come from?" he'd asked out of the blue, and for some reason I hadn't named the town Kate and I shared. "Oh, Kansas," I'd said. "Everest. Up in the East."

"No way. That's where I'm from! Right around there, anyhow. I never saw you, though."

I'd told him I'd grown up somewhere else, "after my mother died," and even that, for some reason, had seemed simple, easy to say. I could talk to this person I didn't know, although he hadn't told me anything except his name.

"Turner," he'd said. "Turner Hays."

As we went downstairs, I'd stayed beside him, and for those few minutes I'd looked at the campus around me as if I'd been given a new pair of eyes. Turner kept leaving the sidewalk and coming back. He kept picking up sticks and dropping them. He was languid in a way that made me happy. Even his body. His hair and skin. He had pale eyes. His clothes were colorless. The corduroy jacket was buff-colored and thin. When he kicked at the leaves we were walking through, they rustled and hissed around his boots. Now he stood outside the Tule. I knew him by the way he moved, the angle of his arm and neck, the slow turn of his head. When he came in I got up to invite him to our table, I don't know why. Kate was saying something, but I jumped up and pushed my way to the bar. "Hi again. Turner?" A sudden longing rose up in me then, the longing to offer him something. He already had a pitcher of the terrible stuff we could drink in that place balanced in the crook of his arm, and he brought it with him and set it down on our table while Kate, who'd been talking, glared at me. Turner moved to the seat across from her. He hung his jacket on a hook attached to the booth. "What's wrong with your leg?" Kate asked him suddenly, which was typical of her. I'd noticed that Turner limped, but I would never have mentioned it. "Nothing. Skiing." He smiled. "I'm not lucky."

Kate put her cigarette out. "Does it like to dance?" She tilted her face when she looked at him.

Already, that first afternoon, I knew I'd offered Turner Hays too much.

Turner told us he'd come to Boulder to ski, but skiing was out of the question now because of his leg. He was in his second year at school. He was living on the floor of

Hugh Pearson's closet, and on whatever money his mother sent.

"You're kidding. Who'd you say? I went out with him."

Turner smiled and went on talking while Kate listened with an attention that was rare in her.

"Why do you sleep on Pearson's floor?"

"In the closet," Turner said again. "Two things about me: I'm not lucky and I don't pay rent."

"And what do you believe in?" Kate asked.

"Disappointment," I heard him say, and Kate laughed.

All winter they danced determinedly, polishing their interpretations of various songs. Sometimes when they danced, they moved to opposite sides of the room like distant communicants, but then they'd come together again. The pulling and pushing of arms and shoulders and legs always drove them together again. Then Turner would take Kate's hand and lead her to the door, and I'd follow them and he'd drive us home. His limp was more pronounced after a night of dancing and he'd walk to the car unevenly. I'd watch Kate look at him out of the side of her eye, as if his high cheekbones and straight mouth, his hands pushing at his pockets, were the only parts of him she understood, or as if the noise and music they'd left behind was the only safe country for them. "There's something sad about him," she told me one night, when we were installed in our dormitory room again. "But what is it?"

"He isn't good enough for you, that's all."

The rooms around us were full of girls who tossed and turned under their college bedspreads, although one girl slept under her boyfriend's jacket, stretching it over her like his soul. Restless and virginal, we wanted tokens of faith, but Turner didn't offer Kate his clothes. He wore white shirts, blue jeans, the old jacket. That was it. And he kept them to himself. The closet he slept in had a folding bamboo door that allowed him privacy and ventilation, and all that winter, after long hours at the Tule, he spent his nights behind it on a pile of laundry, while Kate spent hers in our room.

This was the time I grew close to Isabel, a teacher in the Spanish department who befriended me. "Whenever you need anything," she told me one day after class, "you come to my house. I have a small child, so I'm always there." The invitation struck me as peculiar. She was my teacher. Older. She must have been nearly fifty — too old to have a small child. "Come down to my house…," as if she was the one who needed a friend.

From our dormitory it was a long walk to her quonset hut, past the football field and down a steep slope to the bleak pit of Vetsville, with its miniature sidewalks and families. It was a place built by boys on an empty day after the Second World War, and it was never meant to last. Boys on the GI Bill. But there it stood, in 1966, sheltering Isabel and some veterans left over from Korea. Wet leaves covered the sidewalks in the fall, when I first met Isabel. Then ice covered everything all winter, and water filled the muddy hollows between the quonset huts all spring. I never saw the place in summer. Maybe even Isabel was lovely then, inventing the facts of her life in that invented place, talking about her child and her child's father to the other women as they hung their laundry out on lines in their tiny yards.

It was an easy place to pretend. The first time I walked there, across the campus and down the slope behind the stadium, skirting the picket fences that guarded those yards, I pretended that I belonged to a world where people paid calls on each other. I pretended that I was going to have a normal life. In the evenings, while Kate and Turner danced, I sat on Isabel's hard kitchen chairs drinking Thunderbird wine and talking a little, but mostly listening.

Isabel wasn't married, although she had a daughter who was four years old. She wouldn't tell us who the father was, but I assumed he was important, perhaps in the military. This was my theory because Isabel lived in Vetsville and there was a photograph which she hastily put away when anyone came to visit her. There were other students in her house as well. Beards. Records. Paperback books. She kept vodka in her freezer and served it in sake cups. She signed passes that allowed us to get out of the dormitory overnight, and when we were sick she poured cold vodka sprinkled with pepper down our throats and held us in her arms, pressing a hot water bottle against us and calling shush to her four-year-old, a child she still nursed although there couldn't have been any milk left in her breasts. Eventually I grew dependent on the vodka and the Thunderbird wine that was always being passed around. In the evenings, while Kate and Turner were dancing, talking, falling in love, I sat in front of Isabel's stove. My Spanish book would be lying open on the kitchen table. There would be music in another room, but not the music of Tulagis, with its live band.

"Bring your roommate with you sometime," Isabel said one night.

"She's hard to pin down," I told Isabel, but that night Kate made a rare appearance in the dining room of our dorm. "Where were you all day?" I said, when she sat down with her tray. I suppose I sounded accusatory.

"At the library. Where were you?"

"I went down to Isabel's."

"Who is she exactly, anyway?"

"You'd like her. She's worked in Mexico. She's been all over. She has a little girl.... She said you're welcome to come down if you want. Any time."

"Sure. But right now a bunch of us are planning a protest day. You should get involved."

"For what?"

"Come on! The war."

Our campus had been known as a war college during the Second World War, a place where code-breakers and other military personnel could study Asian languages. After the war it had retained its experts, and it was still a good place to study Japanese, which was what Turner was trying to do. When he wasn't with Kate, he was learning the first alphabet of a new language, *katakana*. Small brush-strokes. A few neat syllables. Of course he had other classes as well. Three days a week I sat next to him in American History. He saved a seat for me when there weren't enough chairs, but he lay back in his with his eyes closed. Sometimes he'd put an arm up and ask Mr. Fisher something. The American Revolution and the Civil War? He didn't see how they were different. Wasn't it always farmers fighting businessmen? His questions weren't really questions. Wasn't business always riding on the back of everybody else? Wasn't capitalism the thing every war was about? How many years had that been going on? For Mr. Fisher, a question at last.

In the afternoons now, people sat at the Tule talking about Johnson and McNamara. They talked about policies and kept track of defeats. "I'm 4-F," someone would announce.

"How'd you pull that?"

"Bad eyes."

"What's wrong with them?"

"I can't see."

"Lucky you."

Turner explained the Asian concept of the Wheel of Fate. "They have forever to win that war."

"Plus territorial imperative," Kate said. "There's no way they can lose on their own ground."

I tried to listen but I found myself watching Turner instead. And hearing his voice. Even while he was talking, drinking his beer from a paper cup, he leaned back against the booth and I listened, but I couldn't concentrate. I went to the library, but the words in my textbooks were becoming less and less distinct. Mr. Fisher had asked us to think about a definition of revolution. How was it different from an insurrection or an insurgency? But all the theories in the world seemed irrelevant. I kept drawing a circle on a piece of paper. Consciousness. The books that lay in front of me were a blur.

"Snow," Kate said. "I hate it. I'm definitely going to live where it's warm." We were leaving the library and the snow that had piled up next to the sidewalk was three feet deep. A few minutes later, when we'd settled around a table near the back of the Tule, Turner said, "I'm taking off this spring. For the break. Anybody coming with me?"

"Destination?" Hugh Pearson asked. He'd brought a Risk board in and there were colored pieces scattered around.

"Open. Florida. Maybe."

"Take Kate," Pearson said. I suppose it was a challenge. Turner turned and put his head on Kate's shoulder and looked up at her. "Your folks wouldn't love me to show you the Keys?"

"Oh, sure," Kate said, putting her face against the top of his head. "I'd be excommunicated."

"That's what you get for dating the bourgeoisie," Pearson said.

"I'm not lucky," Turner agreed. "Nothing's changed."

The snow on the ground got deeper and blacker but it had begun to slide off the roofs by the time the break arrived. The light was beginning to change too, so that the red roofs shimmered when the sun was out and the pine trees that lined the path to our door had dropped their loads of snow and shook restlessly when we passed. We were restless as well, Kate and I, but it was Turner who was leaving. He had a car. "Why don't you come with me?" he said one day in March when we were crossing the campus. "I'm serious. Lily can chaperone."

Kate was annoyed. "You're never serious, Turner. That's the whole problem with you. Why don't you come home with me, meet my folks?"

Turner kicked at the edge of a step. "I'm not ready for that."

Kate was pleased, in spite of herself, because it sounded as if they had a future, something real and sensible, but she said, "I wish you'd figure out what you want, Turner. Maybe it's me you're tired of. Maybe for you love is more complicated than anything else. It's way more complicated than just driving around, sticking your head in the sand; I'm sure of that!"

Turner said, "Don't turn this into a big deal, Katie. You sound like my mother."

Kate turned and ran upstairs to our room. "He's going to

get in trouble," she said, yanking the curtains closed with both hands. "He's messing up...."

"Don't be so hard on him," I said. I put my hand on her arm. "It's spring break. He has a car. He'll be back."

But I was wrong about Turner. I was always wrong about him.

I still had the sandwich in my hand, only one bite gone, and the orange was in my lap. I moved my legs, wrapping them around my bag. The old man was waking up. He opened his puffy eyes and I held out the sandwich, my offering. *"Quiere usted una torta?"* Even as I offered it, I began to peel the orange he'd given me.

"Qué preciosa," he said, reaching to take the food out of my hand. I could feel his giant shoulder against mine, as if he would defend me against the city that waited to receive us. The woman standing in the aisle holding onto the rack put her head against her arm. She was trying to sleep. She leaned against the old man and he leaned against me. I looked out at the desert and the bus driver turned the radio on. Crackling music. A voice exhorting. The music played on as we crossed the desert.

When the sun went down, there were no lights inside the bus. Someone entered with a basket of sweets. The old man bought a packet of cookies and we opened it in the dark and shared it equally. "Are you running away?" the old man asked me quietly, while the sugar melted in my mouth.

"Yes," I told him. "I have done something terrible." I

thought of the Spanish word for pregnant — *embarazada* — but I didn't use it.

"What will you do now?"

"Penance," I said.

"You know," said the old man, blinking one eye, "how the city of Mexico started? It started with people running away from your country. Only it wasn't a country then."

I was thinking about Kate. What did I care then about the city that was my destination? And it would be hard to follow his Spanish, so I put my head back and pretended to sleep, going back to the summer before, when Kate had worked in her father's office, taking piles of papers to the courthouse for him, and I'd got a job at Jenson's. "A long time back," the old man said, slurring his words as if the cookies had intoxicated him, "there was an island in a lake." His hands moved in his lap as if to demonstrate. "This was the home of the Aztecs but they couldn't speak a single word," he said slowly, trying to make the story plain. "They lived without language. But the people listened to their god, who told them to take their belongings and travel south until they found an eagle perched on a nopal cactus. If it is eating a snake, then stop and build a city. Do you under-stand? This happened on an island in the middle of a lake just like the one they had left."

"I'm sorry. My Spanish is very simple."

"It's a pity, but you love Mexico. *Verdad?*"

I nodded politely and looked away. I hadn't expected my first chance to use Spanish would be a bus ride like this, running away from my best friend. The old man tucked his hands in his shirt-sleeves and I went back to my thoughts of the summer before, when Kate and I used to meet for lunch to eat tunafish sandwiches in the dime store. In spite of my assurances, Turner had not come back to school after spring break. We'd finished the year without him, without even a word from him for several weeks. Kate was obviously upset and I began to wonder if she hadn't told me everything.

"Did you sleep with him?"

"I wish I had."

"Quit thinking about him all the time."

"I can't." She said she tried to imagine him lying in the sun somewhere, drinking rum and Coke and listening to music in a bar, but she couldn't extend her imagination past the memory of Turner in Pearson's closet, covering her with his mouth as if she were a meal he couldn't finish and leaving her hungrier than before. "I'm getting a room off campus next fall," she informed me. "Just in case."

"Of what?"

"In case he comes back."

"But you can't let him in! Even at a boarding house the rules are the same, Kate."

"I can try."

I looked down at the paper napkin on my lap and thought about living away from her. All those nights. I'd miss the sight of her brushing her hair or slamming a drawer. I'd miss her moods. I'd miss the influence of her voice. "How's your job?" I asked her, then, to change the subject.

"I hate mine."

"Why? It's so real. Selling things. Supply and demand and capitalist exchange, and all that." Her chin was resting on her hand, but her attention was wandering. Her sandwich was untouched.

"I keep telling people that a dress or something looks good on them when I don't mean a word of it. And they believe me. That's the worst part."

"You're trying to convince people you don't know to buy things you don't like," she laughed. "But everyone's happier, right?"

"You sound like Turner." I didn't want Kate to be so cynical.

She stood up. "I've got to get back." She put enough money under her plate to pay for our sandwiches. "You want to come over tonight?"

That night I took some samples from the cosmetics counter at work and went over to the Hampshires' house. "We're going to bleach our hair," I told her. We had the same coloring; even our features were so alike that, from a distance, we could pass as twins. But of course we weren't the same. She had a family, a home. She was in love. "You go ahead," she said. "I can't do anything like that."

"Why not?"

"He might not know me in the fall."

"He'd know you anywhere," I said. She picked up a cigarette and put her head back and we looked at each other in the mirror. "Your mother's going to have a fit if she smells that cigarette."

"So what?" She pushed my hands away and lit a match. "Lily, what if he finds somebody else?" She looked in the mirror.

"You got a letter. He said he'd be back."

"Not exactly. And that was in June." She'd shown me the letter after work while we waited for the bus. *Dear Kate,* it said, *Don't worry. I'm fine and things are still the way they were for me when we were last together. I, however, am learning something practical called expediency. I have a road to follow in preparation for our life. Remember when you were men-tioning* Magister Ludi. *In a sense I agree with it but he is deal-*

ing in abstracts. Reality for the most part is terrible and trivial, we all sleep eat and defecate. We have bodies and they are separate from our brains. Kate I love you through the trivial and ideal. You are my direction. Please believe in me. T.

"He said he loves you," I reminded her, because I hated it when she was sad.

"I know that," Kate said resolutely. "I memorized it."

Later in the summer, another letter arrived, and this time Kate came to see me at work. It was a sweltering August day and I was working in Lingerie because somebody was on vacation. "It's cold in here! It's freezing! How much air-conditioning do you need to try on underwear? Never mind! I got a letter! Thank you God." She held her hand out, offering up the envelope. "Why aren't you jumping up and down? Come on and let's go have lunch. Do you have money?" She wasn't even carrying a purse. She must have run straight from her father's office. The letter said: *Dear Kate, I called school. They didn't sound too enthused about my coming back. So I'm on probation. Big deal, I'm coming anyway. My main reason is you. Kate, I won't lie, I miss you more than I expected. Meanwhile you have probably become completely self-sufficient. The sun has been shining all the time down here, the water is very warm and the surf has really come up. I wish you could be here, we really would have such a beautiful time. We'll have ours soon though. You just have to put up with me and me alone. So forget the idea of spending any of your affection somewhere else. Please? I can give you a call and tell you what time I'll meet you at Tulagis. Love, T.*

Kate said, "It's going to feel so weird not to even remember him."

I said, "You'd know him anywhere."

But in the fall Turner did not reappear.

We went back to school and Kate moved to her new room, and classes started again. Tulagis was in full swing. There were more protests. There was a picket line in front of registration because the university was involved in military research. That was the rumor. "Any news?" people asked Kate. "Had any word?"

There were scattered reports through the campus grapevine. One was that Turner was broke and living on a beach in Florida. Another was that he'd rented a place in the mountains and was hiding out. "He lost his deferment — that's what I heard," Pearson said.

But Kate stopped listening. She went to classes and went back to her room. She stopped eating, and washing her hair, and took to wrapping a long coat around herself and drifting past Tulagis' front windows with the forlorn hope that she'd see the stain of Turner's shape in the glass.

She had begun to let Hugh Pearson in through her own window at night, and they sat together on the bedspread or under it, in the thin light of the electric clock, and sometimes Kate put her body against his for warmth, but she didn't make love to him. She lay in Pearson's arms but she saved herself for his best friend, and he seemed to understand this. He seemed even to accept it, although sometimes at night she opened her eyes to see him sitting beside her, looking at her intently in the cold glow of the clock.

She'd begun to fear that Turner was truly lost. Lost not only to her but to himself. He had disappeared and the semester was rolling on without him, all its wisdom, all its words going on, so that he would be lost even if he was found again.

One night after dinner Kate and Pearson sat in the living room, where most of the girls were playing bridge, and she asked him what the word Tulagi meant. "It's an island in the Pacific where the guy's son was killed," he said.

Kate stared at her hands. "In the war?"

"Yes." After a few minutes Pearson got up to go, but he indicated, by tilting his head, that he would tap on her window at the usual hour.

Later that night, Kate lay in his arms again, thinking of the distant war, and the distant island. Listening through all the humming and ticking and purring that echoed through the darkness of the house, through the waiting of the females sheltered there, and through the darkness of the hemisphere, for the sound of Turner's car.

Then, while it was still dark and before Pearson had left her bed to crawl through the frosted window to the icy sidewalk, while he still lay on its narrow, unforgiving surface, his long fingers spread on his chest and his forehead, freckled but uncreased, on the pillow she'd brought from home, Kate looked at him and decided that even this resolute bundling, this abstinence in the face of plenty, was faithless. She got up and went out in the hallway to the pay phone, crossing the checkered squares in her socks.

"I need you," she told me. "Move down here, please, I can't be alone. Come and be with me."

So I packed up my books and clothes and moved into Kate's room. We were together again. And Pearson stopped his visits. But at night we lay with our eyes open, listening to the roaring of the clock by her bed, watching its hands move in endless, meaningless circles.

"Go to sleep, Kate. He's not worth it."

"I am asleep."

The semester drifted on. Kate missed classes. She stopped seeing friends. Or she met us at Tulagis, where she sat for hours and drank too much. Winter came. Finals. Then we went home for Christmas, taking the train. It was white, the world we moved through, white on the trees and on the fields beside the train, white on the old mine shafts that covered dark holes in the frozen ground. At home a tree had fallen across the roof of Zozzie's house. I kicked my way through its dead branches and found my key in the bottom of my purse.

"Zozzie?" Go on, I thought. Down the stairs, into the arms of the dark. I thought of my mother, who was down there too, buried on the other side of the wall. "Zozzie?" I pushed my way through the cloth dividers Zozzie had hung long ago. "Zozzie? I'm here!" There wasn't a light on anywhere.

She was sitting at the only table, very straight, with her hands in her lap. I was tempted to bend down and kiss her the way Kate kissed her mother, but Zozzie squinted up and I remembered my mother standing in the doorway, shading her eyes. "It's me," I whispered.

Zozzie patted her knee. "Come in from the cold," she instructed, as if I were a small child, as if she had ever held me on her lap. Then she dropped her head, so that I could see the scalp under her stringy hair. "I'm tired tonight," she said, putting her head on the table and covering it with her hands. She began to cry. She whispered, "I have somewhat against thee, because thou has left thy first love." When Zozzie was upset, she always quoted something.

"Who?"

"Your father, who else?"

I took off my coat. Then I sat down on top of it. "Tell me," I said.

She told me my father had written to her. "Out of the blue," as she put it, to invite me to visit him. "He wants you to meet a woman, Lily Ann. He referred to her as your new mother. But how is that possible when your mother is here, with us? I ask you to give one thought to her."

I thought I had thought of my mother for years. Perhaps I had thought of her long enough. Now my father's invitation was what mattered. I was interested. Pleased. Even flattered. I'd waited so long. I wanted to be a daughter again. Then I remembered something else. Turner Hays had come from my home town.

My father sat with one hand in his new wife's lap, as if her body were a refuge. "It can't be Lily Ann," he said meekly when he saw me at the door, as if he'd never expected me to arrive. They were living in a trailer, on a vacant lot. The same two churches. The train tracks. The creek. "This is Shirley," he announced shyly, holding her hand up to demonstrate her right to him. The trailer had a picture window. I was dripping snow on the carpet and my new, grown body did not recognize this man in the worn shirt and worn face. He hadn't even asked me in. "Take a seat," he said finally, as if the trailer could actually carry us out of this landscape. "Just kick off your boots first."

We sat in the small metal room while Shirley, who had become my stepmother, flitted around the place showing off its assets. Her voice was thin, as if she were blowing through a reed. "We have a kitchen as good as any house," she announced. "The water's so hot it could boil an egg right out of the faucet in this little sink, and the freezer's big enough for a moose —" she paused, rolled her eyes, then opened a closet in the tiny hallway displaying something wrapped in plastic. "Look at this! The collar's mink. Here, run your hand over it." She touched it fondly. "Here. Try it on. It's for you, honey. Oh, it's perfect, isn't it, Biff?"

"No. I couldn't."

"Sure you could. I insist. Don't I, Biff?"

My father nodded. We were exorcizing Mother, I guess, or my grandmother's world, which covered me like the blue coat I'd arrived in and could now shed. Give one thought...I kept hearing Zozzie say. My father took us to lunch in town and drove us out to the co-op where he had a job. I was introduced to the men. I could hear them whispering behind their hands.

Shirley showed me the salon where she washed other people's hair. "I'm a stylist," she said. Then they drove me down to the creek, down to the land we used to farm. There was a house there, after all. "Did you think it blew away?" my father said.

"I thought it burned down." It was true. I had always imagined it as ashes. "All those years I always thought the house was gone."

"Oh, come off it now." My father drew in his breath. It had been twelve years and what did I remember? Not this. Snow everywhere. A door open and creaking like a cricket lost in snow. "Want to take a look at the insides?"

"No." Is the iron bed still there? Or the stove, small, black, made of iron? What shape did it have? Hungry. Round. But I walked down to the window, blemishing the untouched snow. I pressed my face to the cold glass. Peeling wallpaper, a ceiling reeking of moldy plaster, spiderwebs, a bird frozen to the painted floor, a hole in the wall where the stovepipe must have fit. Who was feeding that fire? I turned around in the tracks I had made and looked back at my father, who was sitting in his car, a new Plymouth, with his new wife at his side. They were smoking cigarettes. She looked bored. Their faces confused me and made me feel out of place, but I walked back to the car and got in. "What happened exactly when Mama was killed?" I said. "Did you have a fight with her?"

"You were here. You ought to know."

"I don't remember being there. I remember afterwards, that's all. People saying things about her. But I don't have any picture in my mind. Zozzie said she was running away. Was it from us?"

"She was wild, Lil. She'd went off to a dance and that's the last I saw of her." My father rolled his window down and flicked his cigarette out. It left a small, straight hole in the crust of the snow as it burned its way down, but the air stayed cold around us. "Let's don't open up that old can of worms," he said.

I started to shiver. There was a tree in the yard, solitary, if you could call what surrounded us a yard, but it cast no shadow on the ground. My father was not the way I remembered him, although he had lived on the edge of my mind for years. He was old. Bitter. I thought, poor Lily and her old, gray dad, because I didn't know what else to think. My head was full of questions about my mother, but I said, "Did you ever hear of a boy named Turner Hays? Is his place around here?"

"Annie Tilson's boy?" my father said. "He a friend of yours?"

Yes. No, I thought. I have no friends, except one. No history, except hers. And I don't remember the only thing that ever happened to me. Over there, under that ice as hard as rock, there's water, but it isn't the same water that poured over my feet twelve years ago while I waited for the men to bring my mother up from the creek bottom. The water wet my shoes and went on to the river. The dog waited on the shore. Years passed.

My father got us back on the road and drove along it cautiously. His jovial manner had disappeared. After a while he said, "Let's put it this way. I guess your mother run away for a good time. But the fun run out on her."

I said, "How far's the Tilson place? Could we drive by it?"

"If you was to stop off there," my father muttered, "you'd have to do it by yourself."

We drove on and after ten or fifteen minutes of mutual silence he said, "It was just too much rain and too much liquor, if you want the truth, Lily Ann. Or if not, maybe it was an act of God. Here's the place you're so het up about." He gestured at a tall frame house.

Then I saw the car — Turner's — parked next to the garage. It was unmistakeable — pale and dented from its wanderings. "Don't wait dinner," I said, climbing out and stamping my feet in the cold. "I'll make my way back on my own."

My father turned the headlights on, as if I had brought on the darkness. He coughed and his new wife touched his knee. "As is the mother, so is the daughter," he said. Never mind, I thought, I have something to do. The house — it was very grand for those parts. And the man Kate loved was inside.

As if he'd been waiting, Turner put his arms around me at the door. "I forgot you have people here!" he said. "How'd you know where I was?" He was sucking in his cheeks and looking at me in the new coat with its fur collar — genuine mink. "Your dad?"

"No. But I guess he paid for it. He just got married." I undid the buttons and Turner held out his hands. "Give it here," he said. "I meant, did he tell you where I lived?"

I handed the coat over. I wasn't sure whether I liked it or whether he did or whether, if he did, he liked it on me. I wasn't sure whether he was glad to see me. Had he really forgotten about my origins? The fact that we'd sprung from the same town, the same fields, had always seemed astonishing to me. I began moving around in circles, touching things. "Sort of. Where have you been, anyway? Everyone's wondering." I meant Kate.

"Florida," Turner said, leading the way down a long hall. "But I had to work my way back since the old lady cut me off. She's of the opinion I should make something of myself. Join the army. Join the marines. She likes a man in uniform." Turner pointed to the small lines around his eyes. "See?" he said. "I've aged." In spite of that, he took me into a room that was full of ruffles and lace and introduced me to his mother, who was standing by a picture window, holding a pair of binoculars in small, well-manicured hands. Her hair was the same color as her clothes — champagne.

"I used to live around here," I explained.

"Lily goes to school with me," Turner added.

"Really? I hadn't noticed that you go to school. Why don't you make us a pot of something, T? Since it's too early to drink." She pointed to a chair and invited me to sit down, but Turner kept standing, looking at me. He stood, as if the room were solid and convincing, as if it would not give him away, but once or twice he put his hand against a wall. I sat down. I crossed my legs and smoothed my skirt and smiled but no one said anything. It was as if a common language had never been found for this place with its needlepoint pillows and antique plates. I smiled again. Finally Turner left the room. "Tell me," his mother said then, leaning toward me, "if you knew him at school, tell me, who is this Kate person, anyway? What should I know about her?" She pushed her hair back and then dropped her hands and crossed them in front of her.

"She's the person Turner loves," I said, understanding it for the first time.

"So I would gather. But what does he find in her to love? Is it her influence that caused him to run off from school? Is she stable? What does her father do?"

"I can't make her sound wonderful enough."

Turner's mother frowned. "So," she said, "you have a sense of humor. Anyway, I'll bet you'd love to freshen up. Why don't you come upstairs with me?"

"I'm okay."

"No, come on now, follow me." She got up and crossed

the room and began to climb the stairs, asking me more questions. The stairs cracked as we climbed. We reached a room with a four-poster bed. "You'll be in here," she said.

"Oh no, honestly, thanks, I can't spend the night — I'm at my father's place." I couldn't stay at Turner's, but for a minute I imagined us playing cribbage downstairs in the den — Turner had told me that was what they did, having dinner, drinks — but it was impossible. I would have to go downstairs and put the coat with the mink collar on again.

"Who is your father, exactly? Would I know your people?" Turner's mother was standing in her stocking feet on the edge of a rug, something antique. Her hands were on her hips. The house was full of things that her family had saved up for years, as if old things were better than new. Old ideas. Old arguments. I would send her a note, the way Mrs. Hampshire made Kate do. A little pastel card.... I didn't have a box of them but I could get one and keep it around. I thought then that I might be a person who would have need of such things.

I told her, but I remembered my father's reaction to her name.

"Granger? That's what you said? Oh good heavens, was your mother that girl who died with Joe Malcolm in the creek? I remember it now. And he never even took her seriously. What a shame it had to happen when she didn't even stand a chance with him."

I could hear Zozzie's raspy voice, as if she were sitting on the bed behind me. Give one thought to your mother, give one thought to your mother. Even though I'd been doing that for years. Thinking: at this age she was taking a trip for the first time, or learning to read or dance; I'm different; I'm the same. There was the ring I was allowed to wear. Thinking: at this age she was engaged to someone else, not my father. And what if? Who would I be? Or would I be? At this age she must have been already my mother, think of it, so young. How did she manage? Was she afraid? Proud? Did she do it on purpose? The creation of me. And afterward…what went wrong? Whose fault was it? All my life I'd been charting my mother's life against my own. I hadn't grown into the age of her death, but I was watching for it. "Really. I should go," I interrupted. Just at that moment Turner came into the room. "No, you shouldn't," he said. "I need convincing, don't I. About school, I mean." He was holding a tray with a coffee-pot and three cups on it. "Stay tonight, anyway. I haven't seen anybody for weeks." Months, I wanted to say.

I didn't go back to my father's place that night. I stayed in the four-poster bed at Turner's house and the next day he took me back to my father's to say goodbye. We drove on to the bus station in his mother's convertible. He was wearing a pair of jeans and no shirt. He put the top down. It was cold. Snow began to fall and we were covered in white. He turned the radio up and the old world of my childhood went by.

"Promise me you'll come back," I said.

"For Kate?"

"Yes. But don't tell her I talked you into it."

A few days later Kate was next to me on the train going back to school. I didn't tell her about Turner, that I had found him. She would have him soon enough. They would go back to classes, sit over beer, dance, and celebrate his return. They would hold each other and release each other, and make up their minds that their lives were empty or full. Perhaps Turner would invade the wintry afternoon privacy of our room — the room we shared. He was not allowed there, but perhaps she'd let him in, wanting to learn the slumberous form, thin and strange to her, of the man she had waited for. Perhaps they'd lie together like two similar spoons forgotten after a meal. They'd feel the shapes of themselves, the beginnings and ends of themselves, and listen to the changes in each other's breathing as they moved from conversation to desire. After all this time apart, they'd lie together and I'd have nowhere to go. I'd be an outsider again.

Just as I'd imagined, Turner and Kate took up more or less where they'd left off. Kate found the campus with its sandstone buildings beautiful again. Its every tree, every doorway, every corner turned, was fragrant even in wintertime, and I might have found it fragrant too except that he was too close. To her. He came in through the window — we were on the ground floor — and they lay on her bed and listened to the radio, clothed in the semi-light of ice that covered the glass. And just as I had imagined, one day while they were lying there listening to a broadcast about the bombing of Hanoi, which had already happened and which could not be undone, they made love.

Kate told me everything. She'd waited for this all her life but she felt no joy, no relief, only a thick shame that combined in her with the broadcast, with the sound of a male voice as Turner entered her body slowly, carefully. She told me this. She lifted her legs and pressed them around his back. She clutched at the sheet. She wanted the moment to matter. They lay together, breathing and fitting but sticky, and the voice went on, hushed and alarmed, as the liquid of their two bodies dripped onto Kate's sheet and into the mattress, which had been stained before by other girls with other boys at other times.

They did not go back to their classes. As the afternoon fell into night they listened to the voice on the radio, hearing the subdued analysis. When the bombs had been dropped and the warships had been halted in their positions or moved gently in the gulf, people around the world had waited with their hearts in their mouths. Could they ever take back their innocence? Kate opened Turner's hand and licked his palm. She went from the curve of it to the top of his fingers, licking. This is my taste, she thought. But she had changed. She was not as she had always been.

There was going to be a party to celebrate Turner's return, something warm and private in a cabin high above the college town, and as usual, we were sitting around a table at Tulagis when Turner told us. "Where exactly?" Kate wanted to know. She stubbed out her cigarette and Turner gestured upward, as if the dark women over the bar were included in his plans.

We went to the party in Pearson's graduation Chevy, the beautiful car his parents had given him two years before, four of us in the back seat, two or three more in front. The car leaned around the high turns of the mountain, one door falling open now and then and all of us clutching each other in the clear, cold air. "Fucking door," Pearson kept shouting, "somebody hold that fucking door!"

The campus got smaller as we rose, and the mountain covered itself with black air. I don't remember stars or a moon but I remember Kate and Turner around me as we ascended, the pressure of Turner on one side and Kate on the other, first one weight and then the other as the car threw itself around curves, the view between the shoulders and heads in the front seat, a view of nothing but the road where it was lit by our headlights, black and silver places ahead. We hurtled upwards, the air thinning around us. Someone was on the seat beside Kate, I don't know who, just someone, a girl whose name I never heard.

The party was in a cabin that sat in a bowl of the mountain, surrounded by stones and an old corral. There was a cold fireplace and a pile of sleeping-bags in a filthy corner. There was a lot of dark red Thunderbird wine. Someone built a fire. The wine got passed around, and then a joint. People arrived. People and bottles. Kate and Turner were sitting close to the fireplace and they were as bright as the flames, Turner leaning back against a sleeping-bag and Kate leaning into him. After a while she got up and stood in front of the fire, casting a long shadow on the wall where I stood. She was wearing a red sweater, silver bracelets that I could hear when she moved her hand. She had a bottle. She was drinking out of it. Someone was picking at a guitar and there was a record on. Then Pearson cupped his hand around his mouth and said, "Katie, baby, come over here and make me feel good."

"Shut up, Pearson," Turner growled.

"What's your problem, Hays? Where've you been for the last six months?"

"What's that supposed to mean?"

"Work it out."

Everyone laughed; everyone was listening.

Turner grabbed Kate and pulled her into the next room, where there was a bed. He closed the door and I picked up the bottle she'd left behind. I didn't see her again until later, outside, where she was plunging her hands in the snow and rubbing them on her face.

"Are you okay? Where's your sweater?" She was shaking.

She leaned over as if she felt sick. Then she vomited. There was a stain on the snow. "Oh God, Lily, leave me alone. I'm just drunk. Shit.... Can you…" she laughed, "stand me up and walk me back in? I want Turner. He's what I want. He thinks I was screwing around while he was gone. Go tell him the truth."

Through the window I could see our friends. They were wrapped around each other, dancing or lying in each other's arms, but Turner was still in the closed room. I walked Kate through the pewter trees, pushed the door open, and left her on a sleeping-bag close to the fire. Then I went to the bedroom door and opened it.

The red sweater was on the floor. I put it on. I found the bracelets and they fit my arm. Turner was sleeping on the bed. I moved the blanket back and carefully slipped in.

He was warm. I lay against him. His hands made a warm light on my skin. It was something unknown to me, this light. Even the longing that he brought with him. And his weight. And the taste of him. Light lifting me, his hands, his tongue. I was lying with him and I didn't know whether he knew who I was. For a while I didn't care. I was even glad. For a while I didn't care about anything.

In the morning there were people lying in bundles on the floor around the fireplace, people moving or not moving, groaning, sitting up. Kate was standing at the window in the kitchen watching Turner, who was outside in the old, empty corral. I had left the room before sun up — Kate still asleep on the floor. I had sat down beside her, and stared at the dying fire. Now I joined her at the window. Turner was holding something, swinging it back and forth. A few feet away stood Pearson, leaning oddly, talking. I could see breath, like steam, coming out of him. I watched Turner spin and Pearson throw himself at Turner's back. But Turner dodged. Then he ran over to Pearson's car and hit it with the thing in his hand. A crowbar.

Pearson dived at him and grabbed at it and one of them threw it in the air so that it landed on Pearson's graduation car. Pearson threw himself at Turner but Turner picked the crowbar up and hit the car again. He beat at it. The windshield shattered. There was a shower of crystals, a rain of silicon drops.

"We have to help him" was what Kate said, but she was already running outside and I didn't know which one she meant. The door slammed and I went out after her, the scent of the old, unused corral hitting me and then the glitter of glass on the ground. The snow had melted and rocks were shoving through the frost-damaged field grass. Music was blaring from the windows and the open door, the wonderful music of our generation, as if we were full of the sap that rises after frost, as if we were ready to be tapped. "It's about her," I heard someone say. "Turner's pissed."

"Stoned," someone else announced.

"Pearson joined the marines, man. That's what this is."

"No shit!"

Above this, I heard Kate shouting, "Stop it, you guys!" But Pearson was laughing now, throwing himself at his own car. He climbed on the roof, beating it with his fists until it sagged like a piece of skin. Behind us people poured out of the house. They picked up rakes, shovels, rocks, and began attacking the car, as if they were trying to help. A fender buckled. The side mirror snapped. Shards of glass filled the front seat.

Kate stood there helplessly. We looked at Turner in our

different ways. She turned. Suddenly her face went white, expressionless. I saw that she was looking at me, not at anything else. I was wearing her sweater, her bracelets. I went back inside.

It was Isabel who helped me escape. I went to her with my secret. "I'm leaving school," I told her, sitting down in my coat in her kitchen. The room was warm but I wasn't.

"What's wrong?"

"I'm pregnant."

"Who was it?"

"I have no idea." Let her think what she wanted to think.

"What are you going to do?"

"I don't know. I have to go somewhere no one will know about me."

"You mean you're going to have it?"

"I keep thinking about getting rid of it. Then I start thinking about my mother."

"And you could even go to jail. Or worse – girls can die. It's too dangerous. What about going to Mexico? I know somebody there who could help."

All afternoon we drank coffee, vodka, more vodka. We sat in front of the stove in the kitchen, everything hot then cold then hot again. By the time it was dark and Isabel got up to turn on the light and get Alicia up from her nap, I had the name of the man in Mexico. "He runs an agency," Isabel said. "Go and talk to him before you do anything. I mean he'll take you in, I'm sure of it, if that's what you decide. You can stay with him. You can study Spanish and no one will know why you're there. You can have the baby and give it to someone who will love it the way I love my Alicia. He's the reason I have this little one."

"I thought she was yours."

"She is now. So I was lucky." She opened her blouse so the four-year-old child could have her breast.

Night came and the small lights inside the bus went briefly on, then off again. We climbed into the mountains and then drifted down into the enormous valley of Mexico. The sky was around us, held up by distant hills.

"If they follow you, listen, you can be like the corn boy. As we call him. Do you know how he ran away?"

I looked at the old man's face. It was bruised, sad. "No," I said. "I will try to understand." But it was impossible. I was tired. The bus rocked us in its arms and I closed my eyes.

For a few minutes, in my sleepiness, I tried to imagine that what I was doing was for the best. Giving the baby away wasn't as dangerous as the other thing; that's what Isabel had said. But there was all the time to be lived until then. Lived with it living inside me. Although Mexico was the logical place to be if I changed my mind.

By the next afternoon I was entering the outskirts of Mexico City at last, after so many hours of sitting and waiting, hours of not moving, not stretching, hours of being told one thing or another by the old man. And I was finally afraid. The city was enormous. It wasn't even a city in the normal sense, but a shambles, heaps of clay leaning into streets. Clothes hung on lines overhead. The sharp air. Blaring horns and loudspeakers screaming. A white-faced mime at the intersection where we stopped for a red light, and someone swallowing flames, a fire-eater, who came right up to the window of the bus waiting for a coin to be thrown. I saw him thrust a stick covered in flames down his throat and then pull it out again, still covered in fire. I leaned back against the old man, so that it was he who threw the money through the window. The city seemed to go on and on the way a warren goes on and on, small stores with two or three stories above, iron balconies. Each store had a metal grille across the front. It was a city of clay covered in tin. The grilles were closed, and the shutters. Then even the fire-eater was walking off, his mouth shut tight, and the mime with his white face bowed to us as we pulled away from the intersection. He had eyebrows painted high on his forehead and a round, black mouth.

The city was closed. There were no windows, no doors. "It is the siesta," the old man said. "The houses and buildings are sleeping under their coverings."

At the bus station he lowered himself carefully to the sidewalk. It was our second day together, and our last. He placed a hand over his heart. Goodbye.

I looked around. I was a little afraid. But I had an address and a suitcase to give me weight. A woman standing barefoot with a baby in her arms put her hand out for a coin. Out on the street, I bought a cob of corn with lime and salt. The vendor rushed up the sidewalk after me to give me the change I had forgotten, but I wasn't counting anything. I was looking for a taxi; I'd never hailed one in my life. When one arrived, I gave the driver the address Isabel had written down. He looked surprised. "*Por allá*," I told him, waving my arm, although I had no idea where I was.

He pretended ignorance. "*Dónde?*" he said stupidly, as if he did not understand.

I tried to insist. I had money. I stirred my hand around inside my purse to convince him. He started the taxi and we made some progress up the quiet, sleep-struck street. Even then we had to make two stops so that he could turn around and argue with me. "You don't want to go there, señorita," and "It is not on my route," he said.

"How will I get there, then?"

He put out his hand. "You pay me now," he said.

"*Cuanto?*"

"Ten American dollars." He turned and put a hand over the seat. It was exorbitant but I handed the whole sum to him and he hurtled up alleys and down one-way streets, although he got out once and asked directions again. In a while he glanced back at me and shrugged. It does not exist, this place, he said. "*No existe.*"

"*Sí. Creo que....*" My Spanish was half statement, half conjecture. We drove some more. The driver was silent. Then he turned around to look at me. "*No existe,*" he said.

"*Sí. Son los numeros.*"

"But" — he spoke slowly, in English — "and now it is not here." He pointed to an empty building. Then he went into a small store that was miraculously open and came back with a new address. "It is another town. So now I take you to the bus?"

"*Por favor.*"

In the square of a small town an hour or so away, a boy sat on a low blue stool, blue the color of the sky and the skirt a woman nearby was wearing. The stones of the plaza around the boy were cut into rectangles, with the slight stench of sewage coming through grates, and with the sun streaking across them in patches, and with the delicate pyramid of tools the boy built every morning providing decoration. First he put down a sheet of plastic, then the jars, which were orange and black and red and brown, and which were stacked with brushes and bottles of colored paste and with a Coke bottle balanced on top as the finishing touch.

The boy was hard at work on the shoes of a man who was sitting on a bench with a newspaper in his hand. I was standing across from him, leaning against the tile fountain, examining the crooked town. I'd come only the day before, on the bus from Mexico City that the taxi driver had selected, another bus full of old men whispering while an old woman looked right through me as if I had holes in my dress.

The bus arrived at night. I tumbled out with my bag although another old man had been tempting me to go on to the next town. He was worried about my welfare. He'd been shaking his head for half and hour and urging me in simple syllables to stay on the bus with him although I couldn't understand the name of the town he mentioned. It seemed to be made of many identical syllables. It seemed to be a name I would never understand unless I saw it written down, or unless I sounded it out, and these things were not likely to occur, given the dark bus and the fear I felt. So I hurtled down into the night. I tumbled off the bus at the side of the highway near Tequisquiapan, which was difficult enough, although there was no town by any name in sight.

There were two or three people waiting in the shadows, and there was a car, very small, parked in the watery light from the sky.

I got down, hauling myself and my bag to the shadows, where the car was being enlisted by another girl. I reached out and took the door handle on the driver's side in my hand. "*Espérame.*" Then I climbed in. There were two boys in the front and no meter, no sign that they were for hire. I handed up a piece of paper with my destination written on it and they barely looked at it, but they nodded and started the car. With the bag and my weight pressed against her, the girl was wedged against the other door. We left the highway and entered a terrain of tracks and paths, although there were ditches and bushes on either side of us that seemed to swallow us as we moved.

Suddenly I felt happy. For a little while things would be out of my hands. I liked this feeling of relinquishment. The girl who was squeezed against the door made no sound. She looked as if she'd just come away from a desk somewhere near a busy street, instead of this terrain of bushes and washed stars. She gathered her purse to herself and sat up straight and in the darkness the young men felt the pressure of her movement and turned up a cobbled street. There was no radio in this miniature car and the two boys were silent. There was only the sound of the small tires on the road, and the cry of something far off. There were low stone walls by the road and then there was nothing, only a texture of dark against dark. Nothing was electrified. It was a landscape where houses are made out of the ground and melt back into it at night. This land had been settled for ever but it was liquid.

We were swallowed, sucked up by the leaves. It was the earth turning, the gravity dense here. Your mother, the earth. "Your mother" — a terrible curse in Mexico. The two boys said nothing. I had given myself up to them, that much was clear. The one who was driving kept looking back. After a while he leaned to the left and pulled the wheel and I was more afraid than before. I hated the look of this place. Was there a town anywhere around? *El centro?* Was there something besides this wreck in the wilderness? A gate had grown up out of the cobbles and night, with a path beyond it leading to a dark building. It was low and old and it was placed under the nowhere sky. It was like a liner on the sand, meaningless.

The two boys got out. They pulled our bags to the gate and rang a bell. In a while a woman came out and there were gestures. I could hear her strong voice and then the boys came back to the car and told the other girl to go in. They shook their heads at me and said something I couldn't make out. The other girl translated. "You are not expected," she said in English. "You should come back when the señor is here."

The boys dragged my bag back across the stones. I could hear the bag and the weight of their feet ringing against them. I spread myself out on the seat and opened my knees.

I took a deep breath and the car sped up the cobbled lane. The engine had been purring but now it sang.

This is what the town is like: In the shops they are always washing the floors. Even outside they sweep and wash the ground as if it could be cleaned. There is a permanent damp and the feeling that nothing is ever quite ready. Shall I enter? Or will I make dirty what you are washing? Someone throws a pail of water over the tiles or cement or stones and then there is the ratch of a straw broom.

The sidewalks are narrow, as if once, in an earlier time, smaller creatures walked here. I feel large, caught against the whitewashed walls that go on and on around and around and always come out at the square, which is as open as everything else is closed, as a mirror bounded by tin is open and as the sky here bounded by mountains and sea is open. Women cross the square like birds, their dark *rebozos* wrapped around them. They cross this square day in and day out, with a child wrapped in a rebozo too, and with a net bag dangling from one hand. The men are almost motionless. They walk a little bent, as if ready to fold in, the hat held in one hand. They shuffle slightly, as if they do not own the town. They are gracious. *Gracias.* Even the young ones. There is something soft in the bone. Radios, babies, *dulces*, the pigeons in the square. They have fought in revolutions but they are always ready to go home. They are good at shrugging: Is life nothing but a search for the right death? They speak not with their hands but with their arms, when they speak at all.

Meanwhile the sounds of the women's voices are raised against tile, stucco, linoleum. Sentences that start with "*ya*" or with "*ya no.*" And the radios singing and their high-pitched talk to children. All the hard surfaces that don't absorb these voices; only the children are left to absorb them. In the streets there are always children attached to mothers, grandmothers, grandfathers, as if this is the fate of every child but mine. In front of the church an old woman promised me Our Lady's help at the sound of one hundred centavos. But I was damned nevertheless.

There is always a dog on a roof, barking. The wet smell of the room, wet that leaked onto the corner of a yellow bed in the pension where I stayed. It was the place the boys drove me to that first night. The leak came from a necessary skylight, for the room was dark, with the only window looking out to a dark inner courtyard and covered with a plastic curtain to ensure my privacy. Walls yellow orange and red around a light that hung low on its chain. Copper light. Copper mirror. The linoleum stained near the bed by the leak. Like blood. The ceiling too high to reach all the cobwebs there.

When I woke up in the morning of that second day, I went into town and found a boy to guide me. I wanted to find the agency again, but I did not like to ask questions. On the street there were small houses, hardly houses at all, with open doors and small dark rooms. In one there was only a wooden table and on it tiers of white eggs stacked in flat containers. Nothing else. I heard the boy — my small guide — calling me. Señorita! Come on, hurry up. And I complied. I hurried up the street toward the bridge and the creek that rushed beneath it. But a man stepped out in the path. "Señora," he said. He did not touch my arm.

I looked at him. He was wearing a heavy black poncho and white cotton pants. "*Por favor, señora,*" he said, lisping slightly. There were tears on his face. I wanted to listen but I was already backing away. There was the little boy waiting ahead and my own troubles to be faced.

"The girl is dead. And the baby is crying for milk. *Por favor señora. Ayudame.*"

I took another step back, "Señor. I cannot help. I have nothing. Believe me, I'm not the one for this. There is a place — a place for orphans. You could take the baby there, perhaps? I'm on my way there."

The hand on my arm shook violently but he pulled it away and I felt the harsh wool of his poncho as I moved past him to cross the little stream.

It was a long walk back to the building of the night before, the liner beached in its sandy field, a mile or two outside of town, but for a few centavos the boy led me there and for awhile we were alone on the dusty road. As we approached the place he hung back, holding out his hand for the coins, then running away. The building looked like a piece of dusty, crenelated cake, once pink but turning brown at its crumbling edges. I rang the bell and heard the sound of efficient feet. Tap tap. Tap tap. A woman's hands unlocked the gate.

"I'm supposed to ask for Mr. Hogan." I said this in English, but she nodded and led me up the path and into the somber interior. A man was sitting at a wooden desk but he stood up when the woman brought me into his office. "I expected you," he said, looking at me as if he meant to say, I expected you to be different. I was a runaway, wearing clothes that were too warm for this climate, trying to look decisive. Brave. He was very neat, very pressed. His back seemed to be as starched as his shirt. The windows behind him had wire embedded in the glass.

"They added it during the revolution," Mr. Hogan said, noticing my stare. "This was one of the hidden convents. All of them were closed, you know, except for a few like this. It had secret passages." He looked down at the floor and laughed, without making a sound, as if one of the nuns might be listening from underneath. "Until the thirties no one knew it was here. It lived a secret life. So you see, your secret is safe with us." He gave another silent laugh.

I looked at the blue eyes, white skin. When I was seated across from him, he said, "Tell me what I should know."

I said as calmly as I could, "Isabel Jenkins said you take people in," and handed him the sealed envelope. He turned it over in his hand and picked up a letter opener. "Tell me," he said, laying the envelope on the desk. A slow, southern American voice. Texan, according to Isabel. "How much cash did you bring?"

"I have a hundred dollars. Is that enough?"

"*Más o menos*, if you want to live on the street." He laughed noiselessly again. "On the other hand, I could put you in a decent place." He stood up and walked to the milky window and I could see his expensive suit, even better than one Mr. Hampshire would wear. He told me there was a place in his compound. "Not here," he added, almost regretfully. It was, he said, closer in, closer to town. "What kind of papers did you get?"

"A tourist card."

"No work permit...." He tapped the thin blade of the letter opener against his palm. "Lily. Is that your real name? You'll have two other girls next door. Or, rather, downstairs. For now. Fortunately, someone's just left your apartment. How far along are you? The tourist card's only good for six months...."

"I'd be here a little longer than that...."

"You can go up and get it renewed. You're going to need money, so I'll take your hundred dollars as downpayment for the rent, and we'll give you a little money each week for expenses — you won't need much down here. For the balance you can teach. That should earn your keep for the next six months. You may think it sounds like charity, but charity begins at home, and this is your home now, isn't it?"

I took a deep breath. "Teaching? What is this place?"

"*La Casa Feliz.* That's what I call it. The House of Happiness. It's a good name, isn't it? For an orphanage." He looked away as if he didn't want to embarrass me, but I was so tired, so exhausted by the altitude and by my fear, that I almost fell asleep in his chair. When he came back to the desk, he was padding quietly, as if he was afraid he'd wake me up. He leaned over and picked up a pen, laying the knife down carefully. "If you have no sword, go sell your cloak and buy one," he said. "Here's the papers. All you have to do is sign your name to them."

"To what?"

"An agreement. Just between us. It's expensive, all this, but I know Isabel sent you down here. And she's a special friend to this place so I'm doing the best I can."

I glanced down. The words on the paper were in Spanish, but I squinted dutifully at them. "What's this?"

"Your agreement to let us put the child up for adoption. Your apartment will be ready this afternoon. You'll like it." He indicated a line at the bottom of the paper where he wanted my signature. "Would you like to see the building first, or the children?"

"Children?" I looked at him.

"Don't worry. Not the babies. These are the ones that get

brought to us. They're orphans, more or less. Unwanted. Children of God. I mean, they have brown skin but they are fair in the eyes of the Lord." He came around to my side of the desk. "I'm Gus." He held out a hand. "I want you to use my Christian name."

There was a slight sound behind me, as if the woman who'd brought me in was waiting on the other side of the door. I stood up and reached through the milky light and took hold of Mr. Hogan's hand, which felt as soft as a woman's. "You're lucky," he said. "At least in the meantime you'll have something to do. It's too much thinking that's bad."

But I couldn't think. Part of me was gone, the part I recognized. Not language — I didn't care about that, for who was there to talk to? But something else had been severed. I'd only been away from Kate for three days and most of that time I'd been riding on a bus. Still, I felt different. As if I wasn't responsible any more. I was used to her voice, her opinions, her way of doing things.

Then I was taken into a room with windows that opened out from the bottom like stiff, glass pages, and with thick clay walls and low wooden tables surrounded by small faces and hands. I held my breath for a minute, but they seemed friendly enough. "Their teacher has left them suddenly," the woman in high heels said in English, without smiling. "It happens here, of course. Can you understand?"

"Yes."

"They are being watched all day by someone from upstairs. It is not so good for them." The classroom and its inhabitants made me feel taller, as if I'd grown since entering the building. "There are ten of them in this room," my guide said. Her eyes studied me as if she could see through my thin skin. As if she could see the eleventh child waiting there.

"They seem so old."

"Yes. They are seven or eight. In some cases they are six. Usually it does not take so long. But these *niños* are not special. People in your country like little ones. Especially white ones. So then, we wait until they are old enough — then we find them some place."

"Where are the babies?"

"Oh, upstairs. You will not be in contact with them. But these little ones will be yours each day from eight until noon. So it should be to maintain order first, and speaking only English please." She went to the window and pulled it shut, as if she didn't trust the air.

I knew nothing about children. I had no business teaching them, but in this way I became a teacher. Officially I was a volunteer. Officially they were orphans, although some of them had mothers and fathers like anyone else.

When I was leaving, Mr. Hogan came to the front door with me. He put an arm around my damp shoulder. "The girls here…are like daughters for me. You're like my own family. So if you have any worries…and of course you will…you bring them here to me. No place else. You didn't have time to get yourself a permit," he reminded me, "so we will not want to alert the authorities. Okay?" I thought it was a strange sentence, but I understood what he meant. His hand squeezed my arm.

The old convent door had been replaced by one made of iron and glass. Its window was threaded with wire as fine as thread. I went outside and found my way back to the room in the pension. "We are sorry you have to leave," said the owner knowingly. I suppose they had had girls like me before.

"May I come back for meals?"

"*Claro.*" Of course.

That afternoon I moved to the apartment, all marble and white — the new Mexico. I walked around touching its edges. I lay down on its floor. I made my bed with its sheets. I sat down on its striped sofa, thinking of nothing. There was nothing to think, and nothing to do but wait. There was nothing now but this place, and after that there was nothing but the dark clay room with the small chairs and the faces that filled every hour, waking and sleeping. I tried to understand them. They tried to understand me. Luisa. Juana. Most of them were girls, seven or eight years old. They didn't speak any English. And there was one who didn't speak anything. He didn't even have a name. "They won't want him anywhere," Señora Hidalgo complained, when I asked about him. "Not unless he can speak." She was the one who wore high heels. "I don't know why we took him in. He is too ignorant, he's pure Indian."

Every morning I went into the classroom. The children were already sitting down but they stood up. "Good morning, Miss Lily," they said in unison. I was forbidden to speak Spanish, but by ten o'clock it didn't matter any more; *qué importa?* It was all beyond me. "Your bad Spanish won't do them any good!" Mr. Hogan explained. "And most of them don't speak it anyway. They're Indians. They get dropped on us and we take them in. If they're going to the States, the less trace they have of down here, the better for them." Even so, I was defeated by my own language. They couldn't understand a word I said. Luisa. Juana. Diego. Martita. And the one without a name. "Call him anything," the señora told me. "He won't know the difference." I called him Alexander, to give him a hero's name. I felt as though his silence had been chosen for me.

At night there was the endless barking of the dogs, and

trucks rumbling on the cobbled street built for feet, for carts, for mules. The sidewalks were too narrow for anything but hoofs. I pulled the shutters over my window and put a sweater under the sheet. The bed was cold, and it never got warm even at midday. When I pushed my feet against the sweater there was something there, at least. The air claiming everything. At night I smoked, like Kate, creating a little fire. It was the only heat in the tall room. Sometimes a mosquito plunged around, its sound, like the barking, full of dread.

In the morning I opened my window and looked out at the intersection with its Spanish arch. I was in a room far away from everything, a room with no past — it had never been visited by Turner or Kate. It was possible to furnish this place with a green serape and clay dishes from the market. Even saints. Over the bed there was a niche in the wall, where Mary held a dimpled baby on her lap.

One day I went to the market and saw a toy cradle with a tiny skeleton inside. It frightened me, but I put it out of my mind. I had an apartment with white marble floors. Real marble. And I had a real classroom with children who had real life, if nothing else. Just a little patience, I told myself every morning as I walked to work with my neighbors. One of them was the girl who had been in the taxi with me the night I arrived. She was another American, after all. Another teacher at the orphanage.

"Did you know we were coming to the same place?" I asked her.

"I wasn't thinking about you that night."

"How long will you be here?"

"Until my baby comes."

"How long is that?"

"Five months. More or less."

"Did you come without money? Is that why you have to teach?"

"I thought I had plenty, six hundred, but it wasn't enough."

I was silent.

When we arrived, I greeted the children. I'd been away for the night, but they hadn't left. I hadn't been allowed upstairs but I imagined they each had a simple room, a room once inhabited by a nun. I imagined that Carmen, who lived up there, tucked them in every night. It must be all right up there, among the babies and the other children.

"Good morning, children."

"Good morning Miss Lily. Goodmorning teechur."

"How are you today?"

"I am fine thank you."

I moved between my apartment in Mr. Hogan's compound and my classroom in his school. Two weeks passed. No one had followed me. I went out for lunch in the small pension where I'd stayed that first night, but I didn't go farther than that. I ate, then I went back to the white apartment and lay on the bed and looked at the Virgin hanging over me. She was wearing a long blue dress. I dreamed that I was back at school but nobody recognized me. In the cafeteria a woman put a slice of cheese on my sandwich, placing it there with her teeth. I was looking for Isabel, who would not turn me away. In the dormitory there were two rows of beds and two rows of girls asleep, their feet touching in the middle of the room like the stems of long grasses. They had drawn the curtains over their faces and lay with their heads next to the windowpanes while outside a man washed the glass. I wanted to lie down with these girls, but they would see what I'd done.

"Do you want to walk into town? Do you want company?" My neighbors were longing to be helpful. "Have you seen the shops? They have things you can send home. Baskets. Pottery...."

"No," I said. "I don't want anything."

Now, in the marble-floored apartment, I ate, slept, ate again. I was ravenous. Around me the houses held open their doors and inside, in the dim, there were people doing everything, selling syrups and cloth and string and cigarettes and things nobody wanted and things they were considering. I could swallow it all; I was never full.

In the orphanage the doors were made of iron. I imagined the nuns knocking on them lightly, requesting entrance. On the wall there was a painting of Mickey Mouse. His large ears frightened the children but his red pants with the tail coming through — that made them laugh. They didn't like the mouse but he was part of the wall, part of the time they were spending there, which would not last for ever. "Where do they come from exactly?" I asked Mr. Hogan.

"I told you to call me Gus."

"And where do they go? Where do they end up?"

"It depends. Are you getting used to us here?"

"They don't understand me. Why not speak Spanish? They're already scared enough."

"They don't have a common thread between them. They

speak all kinds of dialects. Good Lord! They speak whatever gibberish they've managed to pick up. English, that's what we hope they're going to need. The ones that are lucky enough."

Around me the streets were alive even when they were empty, for soon a dog would appear and then a three-wheeled cycle driven by a man who was delivering bottles. Sometimes they were empty; sometimes they were full, and there were doorways open, waiting.

After work I walked home and stood in the courtyard of the compound, at the bottom of my stairs. There was a woman, about my age, who lived behind the courtyard wall, but her door was always closed. I stood and looked at it every afternoon. I knew she cleaned our apartments when we were out, but I wondered if the woman and her children were afraid of us, if that was why I never saw her. One day I stood there so long that she finally opened the door. "Hello," I said, trying to sound courteous. "*Buenas dîas.* "I'm trying to learn Spanish. I was wondering...if I could come in and talk."

"I am Tzotzil," she said, "so my Spanish is not any good."

"It doesn't matter. *No importa.*" I didn't know what she meant.

She shrugged. Then she invited me in. While I introduced myself, she threw water out of a bowl and pushed dirt into the water with her broom. Soon there were dark puddles on the floor, the scrape of dry straw against wet cement. Zozzie used to throw wet tea leaves on her linoleum, but Socorro had no tea. She made coffee by throwing ground beans into boiling water. She boiled coffee and water together and the grounds that were left would not attract dust. That afternoon, and for many days after that, she made me coffee. She served it thick and hot with hot, thick milk.

"Where did you come here from?" I asked.

She said she came from a place in the mountains called Zinacatán.

"Where?"

"In Chiapas. In the south. In my beautiful village, where women and men are all wearing the color *rosa*, the color of our sacred flower. My little house — it was so pretty. I lived there with my mother and my six brothers."

"They don't speak Spanish there?"

"Of course not. We have our own language."

"The children at La Casa. They come from places like that?"

"Any place, of course. Even Cuba. Even Guatemala."

"But why? There are so many here in Mexico already."

Socorro made a face. "*Madre!* Who can say? I was working there but the señor sent me here."

"But you still work for him."

"Yes." She paused. "We are fortunate." She shrugged again and looked down. "He was angry because I married. But he lets us use this ground to build our house so I work for him, taking care of the *apartamentos.*" Socorro had lived in the compound — or behind it — for four years, she said. When they poured the cement floor behind the courtyard wall, she said she had sacrificed a chicken, the only life to be lost back there. For Jesús, her husband, who'd never eaten so much of one thing in his life as a whole chicken, it was a sacrifice of value. He'd bought the hen from that stretch of marketplace his own mother called home and it had laid

several eggs before its death. Still, the sacrifice. Socorro
walked from the four corners of the dirt yard to the center
and then sat for a long time with the chicken. When she
held its neck to the earth, it hardly blinked. We exist,
Socorro told me, between two kinds of dust.

Once the cement was poured, Jesús had built the room
around it using corrugated tin and pieces of wood. A room
that wasn't his on ground that wasn't his, but it had received
Socorro's sacrifice, and it was safe enough now for the first
boy to be born in it. When her pains started, Socorro
stopped boiling coffee and lay down on the cement in front
of the stove. It took many hours. All three children were
born on the floor in exactly the same place. Now they were
part of her clothing, one at her breast and two at her wrists,
and when they bothered her she shook her arms as if they
were bracelets she could shake off. When I came to her
room she understood it was because I wanted to learn her
language, but the truth was, I wanted to sit in the room that
was everything. It had a bed and a cupboard and a table and
the stove. High in the corner was a picture of the Virgin of
Guadalupe, who had appeared on a hilltop in Mexico City
in 1531. "Juan Diego, an Indian like me, was the one who
saw her, you know. It was miraculous but she had to prove
a point."

Politely, I asked what that point was.

"It was to show the Spanish people we are children of
God. *También*."

"Of course."

Each time I went to Socorro's room for a conversation, I
left some coins in a dish. There were no windows in the
room where we sat, but there was an opening that led to the
patch of ground where the chicken had lived and where,

later, there were other chickens. The other door led to our courtyard, which Socorro never used but which she kept clean. Around the edge of the courtyard were brilliant bougainvilleas. At the far end was the iron gate. Jesús kept his bicycle in the room where his family lived.

There was another piece of furniture in Socorro's room. It was a sofa, just like mine, which had come out of the lower apartment because my neighbors didn't like it. When Socorro asked me in, I sat on its stripes, close to the table and the covered water jar. "There is a boy at the school," I told her, "who won't talk. I don't know what to do. If he won't talk, no one will adopt him. That's what Señora Hidalgo says."

Socorro frowned. "When we leave our village we lose our way back. It is like losing our name, everything," she said, crossing the small room to stir something on the stove. "So you should find out where he's born."

"What do you mean? I can't talk to him. Señora Hidalgo says he's deaf." I pointed at my ear to demonstrate. Then I covered my mouth with my hand, since I didn't know a word for dumb.

"Maybe he is only sad. When we leave home, we take off the colors of our people and wear city cloth. Like me. But I was crazy, wasn't I? I didn't care if I lost everything. I had to run away from my village when I was twelve because my mother had taken me out of school to be married." She pushed one of the children outside with the back of her hand and went on stirring. "When I came I tried to learn to speak Spanish because I had to understand things. Even before I got hired."

"But this little boy — they think something's wrong with

him." It was hard, with my limited Spanish, to make conversation that had any point to it, but there were things I
needed to know and wanted to understand.

Socorro leaned outside, picked up a pebble, and threw it,
hissing, "*Cállate!*" The child was chasing a hen. The hen was
cackling. The baby was crying. In a minute, Socorro crossed
the room to pick it up off the bed. "Maybe he is not able to
remember who he is. Or maybe he is not able to understand
any language but his own. First you should know where he
came from. Once I said that to the señor, because I know
that a child must have a name. I should know, shouldn't I?
They call me Malinche at home. Malinche, the one who
married outside. But what did they expect? Her own mother sold her to Cortez and now she is the mother of our race.
So I am Indian but my children are mixed. Maybe the little
boy should learn Spanish, not English, if he can't go back to
his place. This is our way to speak to someone from another village. We must have something in common or they can
keep us separate. Can you hold her?" Suddenly the baby was
pushed into my arms. She was heavier than I expected, but
what did I expect? I'd never held a baby in my life. "You
have to talk to him to understand," Socorro said, handing
me a bottle of beef blood to feed her child. "Maybe he is
like the little boy who made the corn grow in a day. Maybe
he is afraid of someone in that place." She didn't use the
name of the orphanage. Instead, she told me the story of the
corn child. Perhaps it was the same story the old man had
tried to tell me on the bus. "You see, a poor man was sowing his field and a boy came by, running because someone
was chasing him. When he saw the farmer sowing the field
he said, if a man comes looking for me, tell him you saw me
when you planted this field of corn. After saying this, he ran

away but the plants grew tall very suddenly. And when the one who was chasing him arrived, he was very mad. He saw the crop ready to be picked and heard that the boy had passed when it was planted and turned back. He thought it was too late. Then the boy was safe."

"I should tell the children stories like that. Or maybe you could come. You used to work there."

"In the kitchen, yes. There was a woman from my village there. That is why I was hired. She was my *comadre* from the village, the one who was working in the señor's house. When she saw me crying she dressed me with her clothes and makeup to look presentable and took me to the señor. I worked first in his house in Mexico City, but then I met Jesús so the señor put me in the school, but then it moved here to this town. I caused too much trouble so he put me with the *apartamentos.*" She looked around and shrugged. "All this way to escape and now I am a wife all the same."

"What kind of trouble?"

"Trouble in the kitchen. There was a woman there, she was trying to get back her own child and I was talking to her."

"So he has rules for you too?"

"Of course. But I didn't know about his rules. He doesn't like men for us. Nothing." She called the two boys over and pushed each child's hand into a bowl of water. "We are supposed to keep our eyes and mouths closed." She covered her mouth as I had earlier and laughed. "Did you understand?"

"Yes." More coins in the dish.

I went back to my room, closed my shutters, and lay on my bed. Like my grandmother, Socorro didn't like the sun

— you shouldn't look at it, she said — so I too lay on a bed that had been warmed by the unexamined sun under a roof that was as hot as a tin pan.

At night I looked up at the mother and the child. Sometimes I dreamed that I had a baby, too. Sometimes I dreamed that it was lost. All night I was looking for it. But in the morning I'd wash and put on my clothes and walk to La Casa.

"Why do you want to learn Spanish?" Socorro asked one day.

I tried to explain. I would go back to school, I would tell my friends that I had come to work and learn the language. It would be my excuse for the long time away. I would try to forget everything.

Socorro pointed a finger at her heart. "*El corazón,*" she said.

She was right. And now I was standing in the middle of a corrugated room with a baby on the way; I had taken what wasn't mine and I had lost my own life. Sooner or later Kate would talk to Isabel. She'd find out what had happened.

"Shall we go to the *tiendita*?" Socorro was saying, and I went with her so I could think about something else. In this neighborhood made of so much adobe, there was a *tienda* where women sat wearing aprons and making *tortillas,* and it sent a particular smell into the street, a smell familiar to the nose of this continent. Corn. Maize.

"*Y cómo te vas? Bien!*" shouted a woman from the back of the place. She told Socorro the news. "*No me digas!*" Socorro said as she waited for her *tortillas* to be weighed. I was in the land of tedium and enchantment.

In the morning on my way to the orphanage I sometimes passed an old man on a white horse. He was very picturesque, with small bags near the saddle, little mesh bags of cilantro or onions, but only the smallest bit, as if the trip into town to sell this handful of stuff would be worth his trouble. He wore a white scarf around his neck and the horse had a few brown speckles here and there, as if he'd been stained by small drops of blood. When I passed him, the old caballero sat up straighter and I always smiled at him. For a few minutes, he made me feel I could bear anything.

Then the classroom would be there, with its thick, cold walls. The birds outside would be quarreling over which branch each would occupy during my lesson.

"Good morning, children."

"Good morning, Miss Lily."

"How are you today? Martita? How are you? Go and wash your hands," I'd say, or "Let's all stand in a line." There was no point to any of it, but it was filling the time. "Yesterday was very sunny but today is very cloudy," I'd say, trying things. "Juana, did you understand?"

"*Sí.*" This was the child that liked me best. She picked up the crayons I dropped, and once she brought me a shell, although I couldn't imagine where she'd found it.

"Say it back to me. Please." I depended on them, their kindness, their tolerance.

"Yesterday was very sunny but today is very cloudy."

"Good. Now, listen. Once there was a boy who was running away from a man. Diego — why was he running?"

"Maybe his father wants to beat him."

"The boy came to a field where a man was planting corn. Alexander — what was the man planting?"

No reply.

"Alexander?"

I had stopped walking home with my downstairs neighbors. They'd made friends with some other girls who were staying in town. They all stuck together. I walked home under the dogs rushing to the edges of their rooftops, and ate my meal at the pension, which had long windows and white curtains that hung to the floor. Beyond the curtains was a garden but the curtains were closed. I suppose the garden might have overwhelmed me, but I sat at a table, alone, and somewhere in another part of the house other women made my food. I could hear their voices shrill and busy with each other, and there was the constant din of a radio. There was the sound of a child, too, insistent about its life. Outside the flowers and trees inhaled oxygen.

Two

In Mexico City there was a building with high walls around it, and iron gates across the drive. It was always closed securely, always locked. This is where Turner stood in March, near the end of the month, at the start of spring break. He had stopped only twice, briefly, to sleep in his car, more worried for it than for himself. He had nothing to declare and they hadn't stopped him at the border. He had an address, nothing else.

When he rang the bell the gates swung open, and he walked stiffly up the long drive. Above him dogs barked mysteriously. He was exhausted. Before he could knock, the door opened slightly, like an envelope, and part of a face peered out at him- a woman's face, sturdy and seasoned. Turner asked for Gus Hogan, pushing his voice up at the end of the name so she'd realize he needed help.

"No está." She said something else as well.

Traffic. Dust. The damp air of an inner courtyard seeping out of the place. Turner had an ear for languages, but he didn't understand. He tried again, louder, as if she were deaf, but her thick arm protruded from the open slice of door and waved him away, pointing across the street to a small café next to a dismal park, her voice behind the door giving the name of the place.

"*La Pluma*". Turner locked his car and left it in front of the hollow building, deserting it for the first time in two days and forcing his legs into an uneasy stride. The neighborhood was crawling with humanity. He stepped over beggers and around thieves. Women holding babies, children clinging to their skirts, vendors hawking things — there was too much of everything. Even the park had trees that wore large, dark leaves covered with a fine layer of dust. Turner had a habit of flexing his hands. He stood on the sidewalk now, in front of a squalid café, opening and closing them. He'd worked Gus Hogan's name and address out of Isabel; but nothing was adding up. He ducked his head and stumbled into a narrow tube of darkness, wondering why Lily would have left school to study Spanish with a man who would drink in a place like this. Something made a sound and he tried to adjust his eyes and ears at the same time. "You want someone?" a man said quietly in foreign English.

Turner stared into the gloom of the place. "I'm looking for Gus Hogan?"

"You the driver? You're late. I know of course you speak Spanish but I will not bother you with my version of this language which is too fast for even the Mexicans, half of which do not speak it because they are Indios pure and simple. *Verdad?*"

"Mine's lousy," Turner said, realizing that this speaker of English and Spanish had mistaken him for someone else, but too tired to correct him. He rubbed his leg with the toe of his boot and was invited to sit down. The man had an open bottle of rum in front of him and a glass full of something orange. Turner looked around. There was no one else in the place. "I am Santos," his host said, putting out a hand.

"Hays," Turner said.

Santos was in his thirties, or maybe he looked younger than he was. He wore a suit and tie, and leaning against his chair was a smooth black stick. "How much time do you have?"

"That depends," Turner said, evasively.

"You are American. What are you doing down here?"

"I'm actually looking for somebody." Turner put his arms out and braced them against the table edge. "At Hogan's school. But it looks empty to me."

The man named Santos allowed himself a grin. "Señor Hogan is away, yes. But I represent him, shall we say. And this is a person of regard to you."

It wasn't a question. Turner said, "I think she's down here with him." He tried to make his voice sound confident.

Santos tapped his glass. "Perhaps she is hiding from you?"

Turner shook his head. "Her name's Lily Granger. Ever heard of her?" He was trying to bring the man into focus. The room they sat in was dark, as if it had never known electricity. He was startled when Santos leaned forward. The voice was quiet. "You are seeking a girl of the name Lily?" This was pronounced poetically. He took a long drink from his glass. "And you have a car? You are willing to drive? The man I am waiting for is not arriving, I think." When he put it down, the liquid clung to the side of the glass. Turner tried to concentrate. There was a noise somewhere behind him, as if someone was there, in the dark. "Yes," he said. It was the kind of place he was used to — a place to drink, to sit at a table and listen to music — but the walls were orange and there were pictures hanging on them, pictures of soccer players and women in ruffled dresses. Turner considered the idea that beauty is not the same everywhere. Santos eyed him. "*Su novia.* What is it in English?"

Turner knew what Santos meant. But he said only: "If she's in any kind of trouble...." He could taste something at the back of his throat. "I'm asking, that's all." There was no bartender. No waiter. He was dry and incredibly tired — he could feel the weight of his eyelids and the force of his beard. He thought of Pearson absently. Suicidal asshole, he thought. As if a war like that would prove anything at all.

The man across from him said something he didn't understand, but Turner suddenly recognized the accent. It was like the ones in Miami. "You're Cuban," he said, and something stirred in him. Cuba — there'd been a time when he'd thought about it constantly. Castro's revolution. He'd almost wanted to join it. It had been the first time he'd thought about politics in any serious way. Now he was sitting with one of them, a person who was part of something important. He envied him. "You guys are working for something, at least," he told the Cuban.

"As you say," the other man said. He seemed to be thinking. "We who work for Cuba know this," he said sadly. "That is to say that it is the future we count on. *Verdad?*"

Turner nodded. He didn't know what the Cuban meant. He would give his shirt for a beer.

"And what about yourself?" The Cuban closed his mouth, like something about to sink.

"I wish you the best, man," Turner said vaguely. "I'd like to look back someday and say I did something. You know, that I made some kind of change."

"Excuse me and I will be proverbial now," the Cuban went on, pulling a cigar from his shirt pocket and rolling it very delicately between his fingers. He sniffed it carefully and stuck it between his teeth. *"Con permiso."* He rolled the last word around in his mouth as if he liked the feel of it as much as the feel of the cigar in his fingers or lips.

"Do you know this person I mentioned? Lily Granger?" Turner bent forward. "What *is* that stuff?" The orange liquid sitting in the glass looked repulsive but he was very thirsty.

"Something for the heart," Santos said. "Carrot juice." He reached in his coat pocket and pulled out a brown glass bottle, pushing it at Turner. Turner pushed it back. "No thanks," he said, standing up. "I need to sleep.... Then I need to find Lily."

"I will help you,..." the Cuban said, "because, amigo, you understand *la futura. Verdad?"*

"Maybe." Turner sat down again. "If you would steer me in the right direction."

Santos drew a small map on a paper napkin and handed it to him. "First you sleep. Wait there for me," he said.

Turner felt his way out to the sunlight like a child coming out of a movie in the middle of a Saturday afternoon. The glare of unreality. In an hour, he had a room with twin beds and a window looking out on the huge empty plaza, the *zócalo*. All roads lead to this, he thought, remembering the mileage signs he'd passed. Pulling off his shirt and opening the windows, he lay down on the cotton bedspread, and threw the pillow on the floor. He was dying for something to drink. Water. There was a pitcher on the dresser but it was bad to drink the water in this place unless it came out of a sealed bottle. In his throat nothing but hard city air, the thin, polluted air of this ancient city. He licked his lips and closed his eyes.

There was a light knock but he didn't rise, he couldn't get up. All this altitude. It was six o'clock. The stores around the *zócalo* were closing, metal clanging, and the sidewalk vendors multiplying, spreading out records, used magazines, rings and bracelets, the Virgin in a thousand guises, towels, spoons, napkin rings. Tamales, ears of corn with salt and lime, tortillas, tacos with beans, anything. Something knocking again. The city opening to night, cars, cabs, roadworkers, a steady stream of tourists rushing to the Bellas Artes, thin trotting dogs and young men going after nothing, *amor*. Shutters shut now, the thin curtains adrift, blowing in corn smell from the street below. Turner falling asleep finally, rolling over, waking up.

The shower didn't have hot water. "Shit," he said, holding his head under the faucet. Still filthy, he went to the lobby four floors down, where a man at the desk handed him a piece of paper. Inside a note said, "I am in the dining room. Santos."

"You have the answer?" said the hotel clerk.

"Where's the dining room?"

"It is excellent."

Turner went up in the elevator. The restaurant and bar were on the seventh floor. For good luck, he thought absently. He liked numbers, he always had. He saw Santos, sitting at a table set for two. Two sides of the dining room were glass. Outside there was a stone wall and the empty heart of the capital. Across the way, the massive cathedral leaned into the pavement, bigger than a small town. It had been built over an ancient Aztec temple and was slowly sinking into it. It felt too close, even across the street.

"You slept," said the Cuban, putting down his fork. He sounded mildly surprised.

"There's no hot water."

"Perhaps," said the Cuban, looking past him, "it is another guest on your pipe."

Turner noticed two businessmen sitting nearby wearing large glasses, slightly tinted. Behind them, through the glass walls, the cathedral pressed against the night. The men had not removed their suit jackets and shot their arms out slightly as they lit cigars. "Mind if I eat something? Is this water okay?" Turner pointed at the pitcher on the table.

Santos smiled. "Chicken?" Then he looked over at the two men. "We will help each other tonight."

"If it's going to get me to where Lily is."

"My friend, it is a matter of saving her, isn't it?"

Turner felt cold. "Saving her?"

Santos nodded. "And I have need of a car, amigo. As I mentioned: you help me and I help you." He did not signal for the waiter but stood up and moved across the room to speak to him. Turner lifted the pitcher, then put it down again. Nothing was quite what it seemed.

"Now there is enough time to wash only," Santos said delicately, when he came back to the table. "To leave, you should bring what you have in the room."

Or did he say "to live," Turner wondered, going down the circling stairs. He'd thrown away the money for the room. Wasted. And he was hungry. There was a well in the center of the hotel — a central courtyard — but the lobby was obscured by a floor of glass bricks on the second level, lit from below like a planet. Red velvet chairs floated there betweeen potted palms. Turner leaned over the wrought-iron rail and gazed down at the illuminated floor. He felt the old urge to fall. Then he found his door, unlocked it, and took a cold shower — there wasn't a drop of hot water.

The Cuban was driving Turner's car. "Where are we going?" Turner asked.

"We are going to find your friend."

"Gus Hogan's at the other end of this?" Turner was trying to pay attention, but he had a headache and the cigar didn't help. His stomach growled. "What's this school of his?"

"We have the tradition of going into places," he heard Santos say. "Your ancestors. Mine also. To go into exile. But here there is no exile because there is no present. So we create the future now in the country of the past."

"Mexico's future or Cuba's?" Turner closed his eyes for a second. For some reason he thought about Kate's skin. He tried to think about Cuba — tried to keep his mind on things. He tried to think about Cuba the way Santos would — "Rubén Dario lived in exile," Santos was saying, "but for Rubén Dario, Paris was the dream and Havana was reality." Turner didn't know who Rubén Dario was. "And the Argentinians took their cows to Paris in order to have Argentinian milk! Tell me, do you read Infante?" The Cuban looked over at him even as the car accelerated, even as he bent forward, pressing on the gas pedal and the steering wheel as if his small weight could compel the car to push on.

"Nope," Turner said, putting an arm out of the window to feel the city as it disappeared behind them, wondering where they were headed. His pack was on the floor in back, next to the Cuban's stick. *To live* you should bring what you have in the room. It was cold. He rolled the window up and stared out, thinking again about Pearson, who was in Florida for the break. He'd wanted to borrow Turner's car — it would be his last chance for a good time. "I'd like to know where exactly we're headed," he said out loud. The landscape was collapsing around them, sprawling into dark places, wattle and daub without feature. Caged windows. Walled houses. A small light here or there signifying nothing. "And what are you doing here? How is this related to Cuba?" Santos sighed audibly. "To you," he said coldly, "Cuba is like a movie, nothing more. But Cuba exists, *verdad?*"

There was a highway sign Turner had seen hundreds of times. *Left lane must exit.* But he always read it wrong: *Left lane must exist.* It was strange to be riding in his own car, but he felt safe. Although he didn't like the Cuban, he wanted to like him. Cuba exists, *verdad?* They passed a gas station on the right but the Cuban didn't stop. "Might be low," Turner suggested, but they sped on across the wasteland, and Turner fell away from it into sleep.

When he looked out again it was beginning to be light, and they were moving across a desert. They had come out of the Sierras while he slept and now they descended to the coast. It was night of the same day but almost morning of the next. Turner put his face against the window. Its smooth surface was more welcome than flesh. I'm okay, he thought. I'm bargaining, that's all. He was hungry but no hungrier than he had been before, and he wanted to piss so the Cuban pulled onto the shoulder of the road, although there was no real shoulder, only a bareness and then a drop. Everything was dark, with only that faint light that lies beneath the horizon. The stars were fading. Turner cupped his penis in his hand, then held it delicately between his thumb and forefinger. He stretched and yawned as he pissed and the sky filled his throat. Without its stars it was almost liquid. He exhaled gratefully and went back to the car. "I'll drive," he said.

"Not at all. I am awake."

Did the Cuban never rest? Turner checked the gauge; the tank was as empty as it had been when he put his head back and closed his eyes. "We could use some gas, man." They pulled out onto the road, the Cuban chewing a cigar and adjusting the rearview mirror for daylight, for nothing but bushes and small trees and the fields around them and a small plane thrumming away, low by the horizon, which Turner could hear but not see in the dim darkness. "Would you give up the past?" the Cuban said, as if they had been talking all night, as if he had spent the whole night defending himself. "You are romantic for a cause. But would you give up your past?"

"Personal or historical?" Turner asked, rubbing his sore leg. "There's stuff I'd lose if I could."

"Believe me about one thing: To find something, you give up everything. Would you do that?"

Turner didn't know. As the sky lightened he looked out at the fields on both sides of the highway. Probably sugar-cane, he thought — something grown by the poor for the rich.

Just beyond Veracruz, a group of men were talking about Turner and his car as if they were worried about the temperament of both. Santos said he thought there were problems with the transmission, or possibly it was the clutch. He said the thing they had to do was *delicado*, that was the word he used and it would depend on the car. And on Turner, of course. They were in a hotel room on the second floor, where they would not be overheard because there was a radio playing loud popular music.

Turner remembered only one thing about Veracruz, something he'd heard over a game of Risk one afternoon at the Tule. This was where Cortez had landed. This was where Cortez had burned his boats in a paroxysm of faith, pitting one god against so many — the god of guns. "We can help each other, *verdad*?" said Santos again, gesturing, palms up, a nice lift to the shoulders. No one else was speaking English, and they didn't wait to hear what Turner said. They went on talking in Spanish. Was all the business in the world done in hotels and bars, when there was warm sand just out of reach?

"Maybe. If it gets me to where Lily is."

There was an open bottle on the nightstand. Two men

sat on a bed in a line of dark jackets. Santos occupied the only chair and Turner was standing, looking out through the open balcony door at the beach and the gray ocean. Santos said, "Take it easy, comrade. Do you want to save your friend or play in the sand?"

"Save her from what?" A ceiling fan rumbled slowly overhead to discourage mosquitoes. No one answered. He realized they weren't sure about him — this American, opening and closing his hands. He wasn't clean; he hadn't shaved. He realized that if he went to the police he couldn't explain anything. He didn't even know their names.

"We drive to Yucatán. And along the way we encounter some very fine marijuana, if that is an interest, it is simple. True, *hombres?*"

"Drugs? That's what this is?" Turner said.

"Does this make a difference?"

"I came here for something else."

"Your girlfriend." The Cuban was like a small boat with a sure direction. But the term seemed to lend Turner some cachet with these older men, with their hard looks and hard glasses of rum. "Is she part of this? Drugs? That what she's doing for you?" His voice sounded strange to him.

"Not personally." The Cuban raised his hands and the other men laughed. Flat and joyless. They laughed to make a point, but what was it? Turner was suddenly indignant. He only had ten days. Actually a week, clear. He had promised Kate to find out what was going on — that much at least — and the week had to include the drive back, which would take three days if the car held out, and that didn't look too promising. "If she's fine, then *bueno,* it's no big deal, whatever's going down with this. But there's still her family. I promised to get in touch with them by now. So

I need to talk to her before I do anything."

But Santos changed tack, as if he'd seen something on shore. He turned to one of the men on the bed and began talking in Spanish. "I'd like to talk to her," Turner said again, too loudly. There was a penknife lying on the bedside table and Santos picked it up and ran his finger over the blade. The act seemed to soothe him. The room was on the second floor of the Hotel Mocambo, which had seen better days. Built to be a casino, it had never been licensed for games of chance. Now it was a useless vestige of the old corruption, even more useless than the casinos in Havana, which had at least served some purpose. They had made a lot of people rich. Even after the revolution, Castro had let them operate. Then one night he'd closed them down — that's what the Cubans said in Miami. They said Miami was the new capital. Of Cuba. Of Latin America. But some people said the Miami syndicate had its hands in everything. Turner wondered if it would be possible to see the lights of Cuba from the balcony of the Mocambo after dark. How many miles? He wasn't too sure about the geography but it must be pretty much right across. Up here, on the second floor, there was a long, covered veranda in the old style, with stairs at each end. He stepped out onto it and drifted to the stairs and nobody stopped him. On the sand, balancing on one foot at a time, he pulled his boots off and then his socks. He carried all this to the water, wincing as it washed over his feet, and stood looking out at the Gulf of Mexico, thinking of Cuba. The thought was like quicksand, pulling him under for a minute. Turner bent down and rinsed his socks in the water of the gulf, lowering them slowly and squeezing them in his fists.

"Why do you need me?" he heard himself ask Santos later that night. They'd eaten dinner with the other men and now he and Santos were sitting in the car, getting stoned.

"Turner," the Cuban said. "What we need is brilliance, *verdad*? But you are a car and a person who can drive it. You can help us. So you can help your girlfriend."

Turner heard his heart thundering. He was sitting in his own car in a strange country with a man who might or might not be involved in a revolution, smoking the best marijuana he had ever tried. Hearing his name spoken by this man in this place warmed Turner. He wanted to ask how, exactly, he might help, but Santos leaned out of the window and spat neatly into the dust. He took a handkerchief out of his breast pocket and dabbed at his mouth. The handkerchief was white and perfectly pressed. "It is nothing dangerous. It is only a school. It is where your friend is. We want you to take something there."

"So I'm delivering drugs to a school."

"I told you. This is not drugs. That is extra, a bonus for you. This is something else. Now we should start."

"I hope it's not guns," Turner said.

Santos smiled. "Why is that?"

"I don't know, man. I'm against them, that's all. I'm against guns completely, in all forms" — Turner looked at the other man — "even if I believed...."

"What, exactly? What do you believe?"

"Nothing much. It's just a thing about killing. Anybody. I couldn't do it." Turner's voice fell away.

"You are privileged to say that."

"How so?"

"It is a belief born out of privilege."

Turner opened the door on the driver's side and put a leg out, as if testing the ground. He was alert for the first time in days. "Yeah? Go on." He had a slight erection.

"You can sit up in your safe country with ideas, friend, but if you have to try a *condición*…to survive for even a day…you will be fast to use a gun. Everyone is based on necessity. Everyone, amigo."

"Not desire?" At that moment Turner thought absent-mindedly that his leg was never going to mend. It would always hurt more or less, reminding him of the friendless weeks he'd stayed in a dark room, watching the aftermath of the assassination on TV: Oswald, Ruby. The endless replays. Over and over. That hurt look on Oswald's face. He'd watched him die. As if they were acquainted, he'd shared that last moment. Then he remembered something else: Oswald had come to Mexico. Like this, Turner thought. To talk to the Cubans. "I don't believe in necessity, I guess."

"*Cómo?*" Santos opened his door too, then slammed it shut. He told Turner to drive south, to follow the shore. "Did you ever kill? Anything?"

"Sure. I did."

"You are good with a gun? A good shot?"

Turner said, "Yeah," and there was a little pride in his voice.

"And I suppose it was beautiful, whatever you killed. It was an act of desire, of course. Not necessity."

"I guess."

Santos lit another joint and passed it across the darkness. He rolled them as thin as matchsticks, not because the grass was scarce, he said, but because he liked the air around the plant. "It's like champagne," he said. They sucked in the night. Outside, beyond the car, the water wasn't black. It was a color without name and it carried no sound, as if on its surface there was no life, as if there was no Cuba out there at all. Turner held the night and the smoke together in his lungs, forcing them down to feed the muscles of his stomach, thighs, calves, his head clearing, the stars, too, sucking up dark air and the smoke of the forests, the green of the continent disappearing into him. Santos talked about Fidel, using the first name. "I'll tell you. This is funny, you'll see, because he was making a speech in Havana from a balcony while tanks rolled by and people were screaming and shouting. You see, he was whipping them up. I was standing behind him. Then he sat on a little chair while the ceremony went on below. Believe me, he was rolling a little car along the rail of the balcony. A little toy car. He was rolling it across the railing and he made that little sound of a motor in his throat. *Vroom vroom vroom.* Like that. Then he was up standing again, speaking to the crowd, shouting and waving his arm." Turner said nothing. But he thought, so, he *knows* him. Santos went on, "It could be they're bored with Cuba now, up where you live. The new interest is Vietnam."

"It's an interest, all right." Turner said.

When he turned away from the gulf it was five o'clock in the morning, and he drove for another hour into vegetation that might have been anything. He was accompanied by nothing but the sound of a small plane, which he noticed as he swung the car around potholes and fallen branches. One of the gears was sticking, but he avoided it. *"Cuba libre!"* he shouted suddenly, gesturing with his left arm, which hung out of the window. He felt excited and yelled the two words into the air, which was neither night nor day. Time was all the dust of the leaves they'd smoked, all the leaves of the branches they'd broken on this journey. Santos put a hand on his arm. "Amigo. This is where you make the future, *verdad?*"

Turner said, "Lily's here?"

"*Quién?*"

"Lily. The girl."

Santos narrowed his eyes. "That is at the other end. You are alone for this, my friend. You understand?" Santos took a sack out of the inside pocket of his jacket and handed it to him quietly. "You'll give this," he said. The rest of his instructions were simple. "You are going to a bad place, amigo, and now you are going to save a life." He straightened his tie and reached behind Turner for the stick. It was all he'd brought with him. When he got out of the car, he walked around it as if he would memorize its shape, or possibly the license plate number.

Turner looked at the landscape. Ahead of him was a village — houses of thatch, a lame goat, a building painted half red, half dirty white, which held the thing he'd come for and which made him feel sleepy and childlike. Then a boy crossed his path, a boy in a torn, filthy shirt.

Turner pulled in at the red and white house. It stood by itself, as if wounded, surrounded by scrub. Out of it, as if by instinct, stepped a woman with a shawl over her head. She had a dark face. Flat. Turner got out of the car to be polite but she gestured him away. She went back into the place alone. Then she came out carrying something wrapped up in dark cloth. The bundle was light, Turner could see that by the way she walked. She didn't look at him, but he put his arms out through the window so as not to cause her alarm by getting out again. Then he remembered: money. He had to give her the sack.

The issue of choice entered his mind like something set to go off. He'd always been free, one way or another, and he'd exercised his freedom relentlessly. It was important to him, as important as being needed, which was at the other end of his spectrum of feelings. But with this in his car he'd be constrained. They'd have a bead on him. Keep things simple, he thought. Don't get rattled down here. They can smell it on your breath when you lose your nerve. He pulled the sack out of the glove compartment.

The woman stood in the dust of the road, just out of reach. She was barefoot, her nose as strong as a man's, her hair and clothing black. She held the bundle close to her chest. When she saw the paper sack come out of the window in Turner's hand she took a step closer, but she put her head down so he couldn't see her face. In one moment she put the bundle into his hands, taking the sack away as if to make the holding easier for him. Turner pulled the thing into the car. It felt soft and stiff at the same time. He laid it down on the other seat. Then it made a noise. When he pulled the wrapping back there was a face — eyes, mouth, nose. A baby, he had no idea how old. He pulled his hand away and yanked at the door. It crossed his mind that it might be dead, but he'd heard it make a noise. He got out of the car and stared around. The door of the red and white place was open — it was a hole in a red and white wall. He took a few steps toward it, but she was gone; he hesitated. He got back in the car and turned it around and started following the road that went out of the village the way he had come. With the baby lying on the seat beside him, he made his way back to the coast road. The baby cried, but its tears weren't blameful or vehement. He couldn't decide why the Cubans hadn't explained things to him or why they hadn't

picked the baby up themselves. Next to him the baby lay on
its back and cried while he tried to concentrate on the rea-
soning of the Cuban men.

Just up and over in the sky was the slice of moon from
yesterday, still there, and the ambiguous sun, about to rise,
ready to bring up the day. The baby was a human being
with its own life, depending on him. Everything he did
from now on would be important. His task was to drive, to
get the baby to the place Santos had mentioned and find the
person he had come all this way to find.

In the morning he stopped at a small house with several
children in the dusty yard and went up it carrying the baby,
tapping on some boards that were nailed together to make
a door. As he had hoped, a woman appeared. "*Excusa me.
Por favor.* This baby. Hungry. Please. Do you have milk?"
He pointed to his own chest.

Oddly, the woman asked no questions. She took the baby
out of his hands and disappeared with it. In a while she was
back. The baby was quiet. Turner had almost forgotten that
wakefulness and silence could coexist in it; it had been crying for hours.

The town Santos had mentioned was south of Mexico
City, eight hours or so from the coast, maybe more. Turner
was exhausted. He could hardly see. Then he saw a pack of
wolves around the car. They were running, one at each tire,
like angels at the four corners of a bed.

Behind La Casa Feliz there was a field, part of the planta-
tion that had provided an infertile corner to the nuns. But
first there were the small streets of a town to negotiate, in
the language of signs and no signs, moving by direction and
smell. Light everywhere, then shadows, following Turner
and growing longer. The angels were gone. Turner was
straight and dry and limed out, vaccinated by the fumes and
dust and uproar of the highway, the terrible metal that hurt
his teeth and ears, the metal of endless transportation, the
transportation of one thing to another, the mechanics of
nourishment and politics, hunger and greed and deliver-
ance. Squinting into the signs, reading the delicate map
Santos had given him, he pulled over. Was anyone following him? There was a uniform but what did it signify? A
guard? A soldier without a gun? He turned up a road that
wound into the weather of fruit trees, sugarcane, a few huts,
the wind blowing around him, and finally an antique adobe
building ahead. He had to avoid the gate, take the longer
detour where there was a drop, a short driveway into a
garage which had a metal door exactly the way Santos had
described it. He rolled the car window up, then down again,
and then the metal door itself climbed up on its tracks and

vanished, as he did, inside a darkness that closed around him. He waited, engine running, controlling himself.

"Hombre!"

Turner jumped. Whatever had found him was unshaved, in a T-shirt and pants. He put a boot up on Turner's window, lacing it while he talked, speaking rapid Spanish. Turner tried saying something. The man put his hand over Turner's mouth. With the other hand he reached across him into the car. Turner held onto the steering wheel. The man growled and Turner smiled weakly back. He didn't mean to cause trouble. He didn't want the thing on his front seat. When a second man opened the passenger door, Turner looked around. He spoke the words again: Lily Granger. *Dónde está?* He knew them by heart.

Three

It was still early. Birds were insistent outside and there was the beginning of that old, gracious light that is part of tropical days. I wasn't even awake; I was still in bed in the apartment with white floors at the edge of town. When I got up it was because I thought I heard Socorro on the landing outside. "*Momento.*" Maybe she was bringing some freshly laid eggs, although I would rather not eat them. I went to the door. I was wearing a nightgown, white with small flowers at the neckline. But it was Mr. Hogan. "Do I intrude?"

I was going to go back to my room for some kind of wrap, but the way he put the question might have made my retreat seem unfriendly. "Not at all." I pulled the door back and invited him in, my hands crossed in front of me, although he didn't glance in my direction but stood by the wicker chair, looking straight ahead. "Now then," he said softly, in that Southern way he had, "I think you'd better tell me a little more about yourself." He sat down. I opened my mouth, but he went on, "And I want the truth. Is someone looking for you? Is it the father of your child?"

"No," I said. It hadn't occurred to me to think of the thing inside me as someone with a father.

"Who is he? Are you hiding from him or protecting

him?" There was something about the way Mr. Hogan looked, with his blue eyes shining and his short hair bristling, that made me want to confide in him, but there was Kate to consider. "I don't know," I said. "I'm not even sure when it happened." It was interesting to think of myself as a woman of such possibilities.

Mr. Hogan looked vaguely disconcerted. "You understand our rules here, though."

I started to answer, although I had nothing in particular to say.

"No intimacies of any kind. No fraternizing. That means with people of the opposite sex or with the locals, Mexicans. It leads to trouble and risks I can't afford to take."

"I don't have any friends here, anyway...."

"Except Socorro."

"Yes, but she works for you. She's part of this place."

Mr. Hogan's hands rested lightly on his knees, as if he didn't want to ruin the creases in his pants. Suddenly he stood up and went to the window. I'd had the shutters closed for the night, but he pulled them open. "How much do you know about me?" he asked abruptly.

"You're from Texas." I didn't want to say anything less obvious than that. What we know about people is not always what they think we know. "Do you want some water or anything?"

He spun around and sat down again, this time on the sofa. "No. Sit down...here...." He touched the place next to his hand and I crept over to it, aware of my thin nightgown and the trouble that had brought me to Mexico. Aware too, in a new way, of what he would have called my condition. "I hope you're not going to take advantage of me," Mr. Hogan said, as if I'd planned on sitting with him in that web of white. "Because let me assure you that my position in this country...it's delicate, in ways you may not understand. That's why I hope I haven't been foolish in taking you in. I found a place for you on my faculty," he emphasized the last word, saying it slowly, "and this nice apartment...simply because of Isabel, although given your situation *vis-à-vis* a work permit, I took a risk...." He shook his head.

I could feel my throat tighten. "I don't mean to take advantage. I appreciate your help."

Mr. Hogan looked at me. There was a patch of red on his left cheek; I could see it out of the corner of my eye. He put his hand out and it hung between us. He had such short hair — a brushcut from the fifties — and pale, pink skin. This quiet voice, so directed at me, was not the voice he used in the office. "You have troubles of your own. I can't ask you to help me, but I guess I would if I could."

I felt very guided, just then, by this voice. "You can, Mr. Hogan."

"I told you to call me Gus," he said. "If you stay here with me, I want you to trust in me and let me help you. Then I'll be able to reciprocate." He dropped his hand and touched mine. "Is that possible for you?"

"I have other girls staying here," Mr. Hogan said, rubbing my finger. "And I take care of them. But you're different. I want to rely on you. I've been watching you and I think you could work with us in a permanent way." He was from home, although I might not have liked him if I'd been there. Still, there was something about his sincerity, given this place and time. Suddenly he brushed his hand over his eyes.

"What's wrong?"

"Nothing. I'm okay. I'm being selfish. You have no one to talk to. And you must have your doubts. You must wonder if you're doing the right thing."

"Sometimes."

"Más o menos."

I laughed, because his Spanish was a way of putting us on the same side.

"You know," he said, lifting his hand to my knee, "you're important to me." He was small, but he was built the way some ex-soldiers are built, as if he had trained too long. I could feel myself blush. I couldn't remember any time I'd spent with a man, like this, in actual conversation. "For a start" — his large hand had left mine and was warm on my thigh — "promise me not to think too much. It's not good for you right now. And if anything bothers you, or anyone comes around, you come straight to me. Promise me that. I want to know about it." He came very close. There was nothing between us but a thin layer of white, and it was transparent now as the sun crawled into the morning room. Mr. Hogan had eyes which had seen things. He moved his hand and I felt my breath shaking solidly inside me. What did I know at that age? I was still waiting; I had no heart for desire, I wanted love. And although the hand was having its effect on me and I said yes and promised, he lifted it and put it away in his own lap.

It was entirely new, this sympathy I felt for Mr. Hogan. I promised myself that my actions, from that moment on, would be irreproachable, although I still couldn't see what he'd reproached me for. "There's one thing," he said as I followed him to the door. He stopped on the landing and looked down into the clean courtyard. The air smelled dusty and warm already. We could hear the traffic moving up and down the road. "I'll have to ask you to stay away from that woman down there," he said, pointing at Socorro's door.

"Why?"

"You've been giving her money. That kind of thing upsets the neighbourhood. You can't be a friend to her without causing her grief, just take my word for it. You could.... This is a small town. I have to insist on this. Keep in mind that you're a visitor."

That afternoon, after work, I walked home by myself. There had been men in Mr. Hogan's office, smoking, talking in low voices, and Señora Hidalgo kept darting into our classrooms as if she were trying to convince herself that we were still there. I was thinking about the orphanage at home, which had been separated from us by a chain-link fence too tall to climb. The fence was a barrier between those orphans and the rest of us, but at Christmas time they unwrapped packages that contained our old shoes and our discarded toys and clothes. I always felt a slice of guilt on Christmas mornings, even though the orphans were no fault of mine. If I keep my baby, I thought, where would we go? We couldn't stay in Mexico, because in Mexico my child would be taught to despise her beginnings. And we couldn't live in America, because America has turned its back on the poor and fatherless. So where would we fit?

The air was thick and sweet. I was on my way home from a job where I worked for no money while I waited for my baby to be born, a baby to give away. I had an apartment reached by climbing a flight of outside stairs. And no one to talk to now without Socorro. That was my life for the time being. When I got hungry I went to the pension and ate *pozole.* I never cooked at home. I didn't know the cuts of meat or the names of things, and in the pension I was surrounded by a family. People talking and laughing. People making sense in another language. *Pozole* is soup made from corn soaked in lime. It's blood-coloured and nourishing.

In this part of town there were jacaranda trees that lined the streets, and a thin perfumed smoke hung over us, giving the sky a bruised, stricken hue. Cutting through the afternoon just before one o'clock, walking under those trees past a splashing fountain, over wet, tiled pavement, around benches and birds toward the street marked by the arch, I watched children darting in and out of doorways, watching me with serious, dark eyes. I put my hand on my small belly and caught my reflection in a piece of window glass. Flattened and smoothed, I still looked like Kate. Then I saw something else — a shape in a metal chair, nothing more, but it stopped my heart and I moved closer to be sure. Turner. Asleep in the sun. He had his head thrown back and his eyes were closed, and I stood there under the long line of trees and held my left wrist in my right hand, feeling its rush of blood. I had a great impulse to turn away, to go back along the bubbling, splashing, noise-filled street — the women arm in arm, the vendors and children — back, even, to the impossible orphanage — and stay there, crouched in a small chair, as resentful and unbelieving as Alexander.

Had Kate sent him? Or was she here? I'd been waiting for something, but not this. Turner falling across my path. Turner sprawled asleep in a sidewalk chair with a growth of beard and thrusting, unwashed hair. I couldn't walk away from him. I was the reason he had come. And he was wrapped in familiarity. In this country I had rights to him I wouldn't have had anywhere else.

He was wearing a white Mexican shirt and white cotton pants, the kind of clothes peasants wear in Mexico, clean and angelic. He was barefoot. There was a pack arranged so he'd wake up if anyone tried to pull it out from under him. One of the straps was coiled around his ankle. Whatever money he had must have been inside. I stood in front of him gazing down. Then I went around behind his chair and put my hand across his eyes. I could feel the back of his skull pressed against my belly. I touched the sockets of his eyes, holding his face inside my hand until he tipped back and I felt him look up at me. "There you are," he said.

It was the hour when everything closes, and the plaza was emptying. I said, "Yes, I'm here." The square was surrounded by shops and a little church. There was a fountain in it, the tiles broken. It must have looked strange to Turner, all of it hanging so heavily in the air while a metal chair held him fastened to the earth. There was an old woman selling string — she hadn't gone home for her siesta. "Tie up!" she called out. A thin dog walked by looking for scraps, and the jacaranda trees were full of birds, so that their branches moved. Then the gates and doors across the shops began to close. There was the slam of metal around us, grilles coming down and padlocks snapping shut, Turner scraping the metal chair, lifting himself out of it. "Your place around here?"

"You must know," I said. "They must have told you. Where's Kate?"

"Staying on campus." Turner pushed his pack along the sidewalk with his foot for a minute, clumsily, then bent over and hoisted it up to his shoulder. He was limping. He touched my arm. "Your grandmother know you're down here?" He'd never met my grandmother but he admired her. He liked what I'd said about her, the stories I saved for special effect. Maybe I'd said too much; my grandmother was a private person. I said, "Did Kate make you come?"

He was walking lopsidedly, carrying the pack. It was a quiet part of town but at this hour a few cars sped past the roundabout. "I wanted to come."

"It's wrong to go barefoot here," I said. "People don't understand doing that if you can afford shoes."

Turner smiled. "What are you doing here, Lily?"

"I'm working, that's all. I got a job. Teaching. In an orphanage. A place for homeless kids."

"Lil, I know what an orphanage is. But you just happened to hear about this one day and the next day decide to walk out of school and come? Without saying anything to anyone?"

"What's so weird about that? You've done it."

"I ran out of money. That was different."

"I like it here," I said stupidly.

"And it's just an orphanage, where you work? That's all?"

"I got the job through Isabel. It's a good way to learn Spanish, that's why. Even though I didn't get a work permit. So I'm not legal here. But Mr. Hogan...." I stopped. "I get a free apartment," I finished, angry at myself for talking so much. I thought of Mr. Hogan's morning visit. He must have known Turner was looking for me; he was warning me.

"I suppose they get a lot of unwanted babies here?" Turner asked.

"I suppose." But I said nothing more, and he put his arm around me. "How about offering me a beer?"

"All I have is water."

"Out of a bottle?"

I laughed. He was actually standing next to me. I was actually walking along a street in Mexico with him, as if I'd expected it all along. "I'm over there," he said. But I could see it at the curb half a block ahead, the old Volkswagen. There were thousands like it in Mexico, but this one belonged to him. It looked more faded than ever, almost colorless, but in that moment of seeing him everything had grown lighter around me. The fountain was behind us but I could hear its water on the tiles as Turner lead the way under the burden of his pack. A policeman stood by the car, staring at its license plate. "I hear the cops here all take bribes," Turner said, as we approached. And I laughed again and stood for a moment, helpless, suspended. It seemed more impossible by the minute. He got in and leaned across the seat to open my door, grinning through the opening at the policeman, who was nothing but a *guardacoche* checking the car. The back was a collection of springs and fabric. The seat had been gone for years. There was a tire. There was the mash of papers and books that went everywhere with him. Old parking tickets, old beer bottles and cigarette packs. "Around that corner," I said. "To the right."

The jacaranda trees spread themselves over us, allowing us to pass. "Right," I pointed. Turner signaled with his arm and pulled the wheel as we came into my neighbourhood — a neighborhood of substance at this corner — everything was a nice creamy color, the street was wide and there were the trees along it. "Right behind you!" I cried, seeing a car in the side mirror. "Right lane!" He swung back to the left just as a gray dog ran into the road from the shelter of the arch.

We felt a jolt and I put my head down while Turner pulled to the curb, got out, and ran across the road. In the mirror I could see him running in reverse. I could see the dog, too, lying in the road. Turner scooped it up and came back shaking his head. "I can't tell," he said.

"Socorro will know what to do." We left the car and ran to the gate. "She lives in back. Let me get the door open. Bring him up the stairs."

"Are there wolves anywhere?" Turner said when I unlocked the metal door and let him in. This was a question he used to ask for no reason at school and now he was standing with a dog in his arms and saying it here, as if announcing that he had really arrived. "Socorro!" I yelled, running back down the stairs. But she didn't answer, and I didn't try to open the door to her part of the property. I wouldn't do that.

When I went back upstairs, Turner was sitting on the sofa and the dog was sitting beside him, looking dazed but content. "It's okay," Turner said. "I told you."

"You said you didn't know."

"I was sure he was okay. We barely grazed him."

"He's yours now," I said.

"Bullshit he is!"

"You're responsible for what you save. It's an old Buddhist rule. You told me that, yourself."

Turner looked up. "How do you know he doesn't belong to somebody?"

"Look at him, he's skin and bones. Down here, nothing belongs to anyone. I christen him Turner. After you."

Turner picked up the dog's paw nervously. "Will you marry me?"

I got Turner some water and he went out to get the pack,

bringing it up the stairs and dragging it across the floor like another, heavier dog. The bag had not been stolen. The dog had not been killed. "I need a garage," he said as he took the glass out of my hand. I watched him drink, a moment of instant familiarity. The way he bent his head to the glass. "Why?"

"The transmission's fucked. I lost third gear."

I took him into the bedroom across from mine. He dragged the bag to a corner, where it lay in a dark heap, and the dog followed him. Turner went to the window and stood looking down on the empty tiles of the courtyard, which was clean and bare, and at the bougainvillea which colored the stucco wall. It climbed and fell and trailed over the chalky surface, throwing its brilliant colors on everything. It climbed up the outside wall of the apartment and up the stairs. He looked down on the iron gate which led into the street and on the wooden door which led into Socorro's space. Then he closed the shutters and stood by the window with his back to it. What was surprising was that he and Kate should have loved each other, they were so different. He'd left home when he was eighteen because he got into trouble. Nothing big: smoking, greasing his hair, selling rubbers. He'd wanted to ski, but more than that he'd wanted to escape. What was surprising was that he should be here. "You shouldn't have come," I said. "It won't do any good." I didn't mean to begin this way, with this tone, but there it was. The dog began to lick himself and then thought better of it. There was a mattress on the floor, covered with the green serape I'd bought at the market. The dog looked at it. I found a bowl and filled it with water and brought it back in.

"Mexico," Turner muttered. He knelt down and touched

the serape, falling onto it and stretching out at his full length. "Couldn't you have run away to Acapulco, at least?"

His feet were black with the dust of his journey and I had a moment's impulse to bend down and wash those feet with my hair. I was in Mexico — where people crawled up the steps of churches and asked forgiveness for their sins, where they prayed to a mother who smiled so kindly at everything — if Kate were there, we could have laughed at it. The apartment would have been full of our laughter. We'd have had names for the other girls. "Fallen women," Kate would have said. I knew Kate better than I knew myself. And love — she was the reason I knew what love was. I knew she'd sent Turner, whatever he said. We were sisters. Not born but made. And she agreed to anything I wanted. The swapping of gum, of blood, of honesty. Anything but this. I went into my own room, where the placid Virgin clung to her swaddled child. Sometimes I touched him just before I went to sleep. He reminded me of Alexander. And of the other one, the one waiting inside me. The bed was old and broken. The mattress swayed. The wardrobe door came open with a breath. The windows let in rain. In this room nothing could be charged against me. I was in the company of saints.

"What do you eat in this marbled hall?" Turner said, leaning into my room. I had closed my shutters and the room in which I lay was dark. I looked up at the Virgin in her blue dress and at the baby with his dangling feet and swallowed something salty, the brine of a bad dream. "I eat in restaurants," I said.

"Let's go eat in one, then. Turner's a hungry dog."

I didn't take him to the pension. We walked in the other direction, through the crowd with its skirts and trousers changed for evening. Girls arm in arm with girls, boys with boys — two circles moving in opposite directions. The older men and women sat on benches on the sidewalks, married, passing time, watching the others, the young, walking around the plaza. Turner and I walked as well, but at a different pace, for we were neither one thing nor the other. "How long have you been gone?" I asked. He was watching some people tossing a ball to a little boy, but he stopped and counted on his fingers, turning my question back. "From you? It's been seven weeks." I had put on a black and white dress — a sundress — and white shoes. Just then the child's ball hit my leg and Turner picked it up. "So if you're finished doing penance or whatever you're doing, I think you should come back with me."

"I'm not." Then he'd known all the time it was me in his bed.

"Doing penance or finished?"

"Take the dog if you need company."

He was wearing jeans again, and boots, not the bare feet, not the white Mexican pants. "I can't leave yet. I have to fix the car."

"Not in this town — they won't have parts. It'll take for ever and if you don't get back to school, you'll get kicked out. You're still on parole. It'll be serious."

"Probation." Turner put the ball on the ground and rolled it to the little boy. "The car's not going to make it home or anywhere else. I need some bread, Lil. How much have you got?"

"Not much."

Turner started walking again. "But you're working. You get paid." He was staring straight ahead.

"I'm mostly a volunteer," I said carefully. "I teach English to little kids."

"Right. To Mexican orphans. That makes a lot of sense."

"For when they get adopted by people in the States. If you start getting nosy, you'll get me in trouble. So just don't, please." Trouble. I was already there. My belly was almost breathing.

"Well, it so happens that I've met the people you work for, and I think what they're doing could be illegal."

"Meaning what?"

"Buying babies."

"Turner! I don't know what you heard, but don't start imagining things."

Turner shook his head as if he were trying to get something out of it. "Okay, let's find something to eat." Neither of us mentioned Kate, but I decided I didn't care. Not that night. We were a thousand miles away from her. We were going to a restaurant where we could sit on painted chairs and eat until we weren't hungry anymore.

"Más cerveza?" a woman shouted from the kitchen an hour later, when we had lifted the last spoonfuls of *mole poblano* into our mouths. We could hear the broom moving across the scratchy floor. She probably wanted to come out and sit in front of her restaurant and watch the couples walking on the plaza, but she didn't know how we'd feel about that. We were gringos. We might need more service. I'd seen her sitting outside before with her grownup sons, watching the young girls of the neighborhood watch her boys out of the corners of their eyes. Some of the girls were light-haired. The *criollos* were the Spanish born to Mexico. The pastel buildings they made were all around us, thick and cool and crumbling. The gods they invented were half new, half old. "We have to find you a place to stay," I told Turner.

He put his fork down. "You must be kidding. It's not like you only have one bed."

I watched him to see what he felt. "We're not allowed to have men stay over," I said.

"Who's we?"

"The other girls…who work with me."

"Then I'll sleep in my car. But remember what you said about being responsible for what you save."

"I haven't saved you."

Turner lifted his hand as the woman who ran the restaurant came out of the kitchen to stand in the doorway with her broom. "Yes you have."

I remembered the night Socorro and Jesús had brought me here. When we sat on the benches outside and watched the girls and boys passing in their counterrevolutions. Little insurgencies. I'd asked Jesús if he would bring us out three beers from the restaurant and he'd done it but he hadn't liked it, I could tell. He liked to sit at a table. A table was the place for beer. We weren't able to go into the place, though, not the three of us. We weren't comfortable with that idea. I remembered the señora from that night, the señora and her grownup sons. Socorro had carried her smallest child in her rebozo but she'd left the two boys at home. "And if there is a fire from the gas?" Jesús wanted to know. *"Madre de Dios,"* Socorro answered, crossing herself and rushing forward, plunging toward the little plaza where we were to sit in order to be done with it. Then we sat with our bottles at our feet in the dust after each swallow, thinking of fire as the boys circled the girls. If there had been mariachis, I would have held the baby and told Socorro and Jesús to dance. They were strangers here too. She had come from the mountains, from her mother's mud house, and Jesús had come out of nowhere, from the marketplace and the folds of his mother's skirt.

"Ask me," Turner said quietly.

"What?"

"What you saved me from."

"I don't care."

"Why's that?"

"I just don't."

Turner pushed up from the table without touching it, scraping his chair back. He smelled of sweat and there was the faint sound of music a block or two away. The girls were passing. They were pretty in their shawls, and they looked at him. I bought some beer to take home with us, and the bottles rang at our sides like bells when we walked. All the way through the dark and light streets, they rang. The dog trotted along too, all the way to the arch that was erected long ago to commemorate the arrival of a Spanish viceroy. Turner said, "Who's the guy downstairs from you, if men aren't allowed?"

"Oh, Jesús. Socorro's husband." A small boy darted out of the shadows and paused. I reached in the pocket of my skirt, where I always kept coins. The little hand reached out but I wasn't looking and the coins scattered all over the pavement in the darkness. We could hear them, metal against stone. Scissors paper rock. Turner reached down to look for them. The boy waited silently, his hand held up, the open palm. We had come to the boulevard of jacarandas, and they bent over us, ruffling the leaves stitched to their dark branches. Turner thrust the coins back at the child. "You shouldn't teach them to beg," he said. "They learn to sell themselves that way."

"I'll come in and get my toothbrush," he said, as we reached my gate, "but don't worry. Dog and I will sleep outside. I'll catch Jesus or whatever his name is in the morning."

"For what?"

"So he can help me sell something. If you don't have any money, I'll raise it myself."

"Sell what? Turner, if it's dope or something, don't be stupid. You'll end up in a Mexican jail."

Turner yawned. "It's going to be uncomfortable sleeping on that damned tire."

"Okay, you can stay for tonight. But I don't want any-body seeing you." We opened the iron gate like thieves; even the dog was quiet when we went up the metal stairs. Turner went to sleep again and I sat on the sofa reading a Donald Lam and Bertha Cool mystery. It was the only book in the apartment except for a mystery about de Gaulle. I wondered if the last inhabitant had been a slower reader than I was, or if she'd taken some books away with her. Books, but no child. I imagined her wrapping them up in a blanket, cradling them in her arms. When I got sleepy, I brushed my hair a hundred times for my grandmother. Sweep, sweep like the señora waiting to regain the night.

"Pearson got his orders," Turner said the next morning. "Did I tell you that yet?" He came out of my kitchen gnawing on a piece of bread, wearing no shirt, no shoes. "He's going to Vietnam. 'Deployed,' as he says."

"When?"

"This June." He brushed some crumbs off his chest.

"Is he scared?"

"He's out of his head. Too much acid or something. He thinks he can't die."

"What about the people over there?"

"For him, they don't even come into it. Is that Socorro's old man? What's his name, Jesus?"

"Jesús." I pronounced it correctly and looked down. Jesús was below us in the courtyard, pushing his bicycle to the gate.

"I need to talk to him," Turner said, starting for the door.

"Turner, don't. You promised. I'll get in trouble if they find out you're in here."

"How? They that uptight?" He went into the room where he'd slept. Then he went outside, halfway down the stairs, and leaned against the wall with his eyes closed, waiting for Jesús. In the courtyard there were still shadows. It was only seven o'clock. Jesús might come back any minute. He had many little jobs because he owned a bicycle. He mounted it several times a day to run an errand or make a small delivery, while the chickens in the back pecked at the grain Socorro threw at them.

"Turner, please. Come in!"

Turner stood on the stairs. The other girls would be up by now, getting dressed, getting ready to walk to La Casa — although one didn' t have much longer here. Her baby was due in a month and then she would disappear and there would be another child upstairs at La Casa. "Turner?" It was no use. I had to leave him there and go off to the orphanage.

"I don't get it," Turner said that night over a platter of shrimp. "You're in the middle of school. You don't need a job. We could have talked. Not involved Kate. It happened. But you suddenly run off down here." He was chewing while he talked, something my grandmother could not abide. "Why'd you have to go away without telling us?"

The dog was at our feet. I was feeding it pieces of bread under the table. I said, "You tell me first. Why'd you come? Was it for Kate?"

"I came for you." He was splitting shells with his thumbs. The señora was tucked into the big kitchen with her sons. I could hear her throaty laugh as Turner arranged shells on the platter, lining up a transparent battalion. Then he looked up. "So what about it? Is this all you want from life or will you come back to school?"

"I can't."

"Why not?"

"I signed a contract. I'll go back next year."

"I thought you liked school. You were the only one of us who did. You think you can learn Spanish better here than in a nice, clean classroom?"

I laughed. "I have a little boy who won't say a word in my class," I said. "Nothing I do works for him." That very morning I had taken myself to the table where Alexander sat. It was so low that I towered over it. "Good morning," I'd said to Alexander. "How are you today?"

His look had begged me to let him be.

"Good morning, children," I'd said in my father's English, to the whimpering children as well as to the stalwart ones. "Good morning!" the children had chanted back. All except Alexander, who sat looking at his feet. I told Turner how Alexander's dark face was like putty, how all the faces orbited around me; how lonely I was; it was such a relief to say these things. I couldn't admit them to the other girls. "Luisa started shouting," I said. "Right when I was trying to get Alexander to talk. Julia grabbed the charm she wears around her neck and wouldn't let go of it."

Turner interrupted. "You really care about all this?"

What choice did I have? I wasn't thinking about the children so much. What I kept thinking about was the mothers. I could talk to the children, teach them things, but their mothers would never see them again. To save the morning I'd asked the children to draw a picture of a house. I'd tried to demonstrate, using my hands in the air. I'd given them large pieces of soft yellow paper. Most of them drew a square. But Alexander drew a circle. The children teased him. "Look!" Juana had said in Spanish, pointing, "He made a hole!" Diego said, "Now he can piss in it!" "That's all he ever does," another one shouted, "piss and pick his nose!" One of them had grabbed the paper and ripped it in half.

The dog stood up and stretched. The señora approached our table with her tray and a damp rag. The night waited outside, full and gathering more fullness. Turner leaned against me, as if he needed help, my shoes clicking on the street. "Señora señora," said a small boy, tugging at his short pants shyly, one hand out. *"Dame?"* Give to me. It was miraculous how many coins there were, and how many children, also miracles. They came out of the unlit street corners whispering and nudging while the dog moved ahead, slightly afraid of them.

How to draw a house: Draw two hills that meet in the middle of the paper. Put a sun between them so that it is setting. Make rays around it. Use yellow. Outline a house on one of the hills. Put a chimney on the house with smoke. Use red for the chimney. Use green for the hills. Color the house brown or white. It has four windows and a door. A father and mother and child. Turner and I walked through the dark streets of a dark neighborhood in the middle of nowhere. Four rooms were waiting in the darkness. The dog was shadowing us; his shadow and ours moved along the pavement. We'd left Los Arcos, an arch that turned the god Quetzalcoatl into a man. You see, said the Spanish to the Indians, here is your god, but he is ordinary. Look at him. We were passing the *zócalo*, the most important part of any town — more important than the church, more important than the marketplace. In the *zócalo* the Mexican looks for communion. Even before the Spanish came, the Indians had these centers of ceremony. That night with Turner in Tequisquiapan there were scores of people, scores of dogs, dozens of little boys looking for a few centavos. They were not home in bed, those little ones, because they had no beds, or because they were with mothers who stood in darker streets. They tugged at my sleeves as if they were asking for a benediction. As if it were due to them.

A few blocks away there was a cantina, and Turner and I went to it and sat within reach of the door. We drank warm cerveza because that was all they served after the ice melted in the tub where the bottles were stored. We didn't care. The dog lay between us under our feet and we ate again, this time tortillas that were warm in our hands. I bought a pair of tiny earrings from a woman with a tray of them. "But you don't have pierced ears," Turner protested.

"I'll get them," I said, feeling slightly faint.

"You all right?"

I put my head down. "The other girls are always warning me not to eat anything on the street." As if it mattered that we take care of ourselves. There was a rumor that one of the girls had bought food from every vendor, off every cart. She ate everything and she got sick all the time. But she was still pregnant. There was only one cure for what was wrong with us and it was too terrible to think about.

Turner took hold of my hand. "There's something wrong about that place you work," he said. "I can't figure it out. It seems to be connected to Cubans, but I can't see how."

I wanted to laugh, but I felt too miserable. "What Cubans?" I asked weakly, trying to clear my head. "Gus Hogan is as Texan as they come." A man was approaching our table, holding out a dark red flower. He wanted Turner to buy it for me, but Turner said, "It was Cubans who knew where you were. A guy named Santos and a couple of others and I did something terrible for them in order to get to you. I don't even want to think about it. But I wasn't prepared — it just happened. It happened in some nameless hole down the coast. I didn't have time to get out of it."

"What'd you do?"

Turner told me. All of it. I said, "Turner, you're crazy.

What a crazy thing to do!"

"It was terrible. I took a baby right out of its mother's arms, Lily. She sold it to me."

"Why'd you do it?"

"I was trying to find you. They asked me to do something in exchange." Turner stood up and ducked his head, although the doorway was tall enough.

"Gus Hogan helps people," I said, trying to catch up. "And you don't know for sure what the situation was. It's not like you kidnapped anyone."

But Turner was crashing against the night. He was banging against the outside tables and chairs. He didn't believe me. I knew the look on his face even when it was turned away. So I held his hands.

We climbed the stairs. Alone in a foreign country, we spoke the language we had in common. The silences in his hands and mine rubbed together, producing something. We entered a room without weather, but we brought weather inside with us. We didn't turn on the lights, the shutters were open. The night came through the door with us but some of it was waiting anyway. I took Turner into the second bedroom of my apartment for the second time. The other one had a real bed, but we didn't go in there under the eyes of the Virgin. We were full of beer. Our tired legs felt unsuitable. We dropped to the mattress on the floor. "How did you do this to me?" I asked. It was my only question and I was finally asking it, but Turner didn't understand. He lay on his back looking up, his arms flat at his sides. Then he said, "Give me your hand," and lifted it to his face.

I think it began to rain, the tile roof absorbing noise. Once I had stood outside on a cold night in the mountains, having drunk the right amount of Thunderbird and having come out there with my best friend. She was beside me, but what I wanted was inside. The door opened. I wanted to be on the other side of it. The wine had mixed with my blood and I walked into a room where I didn't belong and lay down on a bed that wasn't mine. I pushed myself against the man Kate loved, against the smell of his skin. And now I was holding him, kissing him. I was possessing his mouth with or without words. The night settled around us like a blanket and the serape provided its rough surface under us.

Dear Kate,
Today I hit a dog which upset me very much however it is all right, but my headlight got smashed. Also the transmission is messed up but don't worry I'm getting it fixed. Kate I miss you. Otherwise things are fine. I saw Lily but she got a job here so she won't come back. You'll see me before you get this. Anyway keep the faith. I don't know what will become of me if you don't —

There were thirty-three children sleeping upstairs at La Casa, including the babies we weren't allowed to see. A week before there had been thirty-eight but now there were thirty-three, as there were thirty-three years in Christ's life. And in Alexander the Great's. And where had they come from, all those children? Martita — she was brought in by a grandmother who was sick, who said, "Take her before I take myself to bed." Or was it somebody else who brought her? Señora Hidalgo didn't keep many records. When I got to work that day, Martita was sitting by the desk in the outer office and through the door I could see some men looking serious around Mr. Hogan's desk. As if there was an understanding among them, they were nodding their heads. Martita had her little finger in her mouth. That was the one she always sucked, for some reason. Her nose was running but her dress was clean. It was the dress she'd arrived in, blue with braid at the hem and a sash at the waist, the same dress she wore every day. *"Martita ven aqui. Tu camisa...."* I didn't know the word for sash but I held out my hands.

"English," said Señora Hidalgo. She was opening a drawer.

"Come here," I said to Martita. "Let me tie your dress." But Martita hung her head. Her bare feet dangled from the little chair. I could see the top of her head, her stubby knees, her ten toes, her thin arms. Sometimes this little one, the youngest of all, looked around at us as if she was wondering where the familiar hands and faces and voices had gone. At night they put chairs around her cot so she wouldn't fall out. Or climb.

"Señora," I said. "I need some money for expenses."

Señora Hidalgo turned, her high-heeled shoes soft on the tiles like a sponge. She lifted her eyebrows and shook her head, tipping it in the direction of Mr. Hogan's door. The drawer was open in front of her, but she slammed it lightly, there was so little in it. "How is it financed, this place?" I said then, putting it that way around because I thought she'd understand my English words better if they were reversed. Also I was embarrassed about asking for the advance. Now that Turner had come I was spending all my money. "It is not an agency of the government, so how is it paying for itself?"

"Private," she said. "Adoptions."

"People pay for children?" I suppose it was obvious but it had never crossed my mind. I looked at Martita's bowed head. "But how many got adopted this year? It can't be very many." I could see Mr. Hogan at his wooden desk. Then he called out, "Señora, please send her in."

I stood up, but Señora Hidalgo pulled Martita off the chair and brought her across the outer office to Mr. Hogan's door. She pushed the little girl inside and stepped back, pulling the door shut behind her. "You should go in to your room," Señora Hidalgo reminded me, but this time I was the one who shook my head. "Martita. She's one of mine," I said.

Señora Hidalgo didn't know what to say. She moved some things around on her desk and tapped her foot. In a minute she got up abruptly and swept out of the room. She was going to have to bring order to my students herself.

Half an hour went by. Then Mr. Hogan's door opened and he stood there, in its frame. He looked surprised. "You," he said. "You're waiting for me? Please come in."

There were men in the room, but there was no sign of Martita. She'd disappeared. Maybe she'd gone out one of the secret entrances. "Where's Martita?"

"I thought you said no one was looking for you," Mr. Hogan said. There was a small sneer in his voice. "So who spent the night at your place? The father of your baby? Or just a casual lay?"

I looked at him in surprise. I said, "He's my best friend's boyfriend," but that was the moment I realized what I'd done. I'd come to Mexico to avoid Turner, to get away from him and the thing he and I had started, but now I'd swallowed him. I put my hand over my belly and leaned forward, wishing to be sick, feeling sick, terrible, full of Turner for ever. I hadn't even thought of Kate when I got up off the green serape and unwrapped myself from him. There was no end to this unless I rushed back and declared my regret.

What ties did I have to the world? Only two. Kate and Zozzie. Turner couldn't come into it.

The men were staring at me. Mr. Hogan picked at a small scab on his hand. He had the look of a middle-aged man, and sadness in that place between eyes and ears where sadness collects. He had perfect hands, but there was a scab on one of them.

"Where's Martita?" I asked again.

"She's gone. Someone came for her. I want that boy out of my place, Lily. There are rules here and you agreed to abide by them."

"His car broke down."

"That's no concern of yours. You take on the troubles of the world and you end up carrying them around for nine months." Mr. Hogan stood up, came around the desk, put a hand under my chin, and tipped my head back so that I was looking up. "I thought you were going to help me here."

By one o'clock I was back at the apartment. Jesús and Turner were standing in the tiled courtyard, the colors of the bougainvillea as brilliant as flags around them, but Turner could feel me arrive. I saw him look up while I was still across the street, and he seemed to lose interest in Jesús. He turned and I could feel it right through the bars. In a minute I stood on the red, lined squares that surrounded him, that made the ground under his feet extend all the way to my body. "I have to talk to you."

"Jesús, man, my pleasure. *Hasta luego.*"

I was climbing the stairs just ahead of him. I could feel his breath on my thigh.

"Where were you? It's afternoon. I woke up and missed you."

I pulled the door open. There was the cold floor, the face, the hands, the weight of his body, the string through the cloth. Desire. "Why is it so dark?"

"It's going to storm."

It was only March, but the sky was turning green with the insignia of heat, as if we had pulled it there ourselves. Green light jolted from one corner to another of everything visible — light, dark, light — and then rain hit the street and the ground outside, battering earth and trees, shattering the pavement while we rolled under it as beaten as creatures with wings, while I folded myself into the cave of Turner's flesh, forcing his bones apart and crawling out again.

Afterwards we lay on the marble floor, empty, back in the region of solitude that is the only country bodies really inhabit. I rolled away from Turner, feeling my bones on the tiles, telling myself to go into the kitchen, put a pot of water on to boil, light the gas for a bath, and wash. Then I remembered: I must forget Turner. Before anything else. I must forget my new skin, I must tell him to leave, this had to stop. "Listen...."

"Wait. I know I have to go. But help me out with some money first, before you throw me out."

"Right now? You're leaving? I'm just getting up to cook some shrimp."

"That's all you ever eat. We're going to share a meal tonight with Jesús and his lady. I already asked them. He's working on some contacts for me. Then the car. Then I want you to leave with me."

"Aren't you forgetting something?"

"What?"

"Kate."

"I'm not forgetting her. We'll talk about that."

"First I need a bath. Do people always smell like this afterward?"

"I think so. I'm not an expert."

"Mr. Hogan knows you're here."

"He should, after I bought a baby for his orphanage." Turner got up off the floor and walked over to the window. "We have to get out of here, Lil."

We went for a walk in the rain. When we were soaked, we stopped for coffee in a café. What does the language say? *A sus órdenes:* at your orders. *Para servirle:* to serve you. *Cómo no:* how not. Yes, it is clear that yes: *claro que sí.* Demand of me: *mande.* Turner was trying to order coffee. He was tapping the side of his cup with a spoon, which was the custom in that place. We'd walked all the way to the *zócalo,* which was surrounded by covered verandas outside restaurants and shops. When we sat down, a small boy came up and put an onyx elephant on the table in front of us. Turner kept tapping on his cup; we'd been given coffee but no milk. Another elephant appeared. *Para servirle.* "The waiter, where is he?" Turner said. I was listening to the sound of the rain and watching the boy with the onyx elephants. A fan was swinging around and a table near us was full of men; one had his son with him. They were all drinking coffee except for the son, who had a bottle of Coke. When he'd finished drinking it, the father gave him some money and sent him off. The men were enjoying themselves. The elephants were still coming. We still had coffee but no hot milk. There was a newsstand just outside, and a girl leaned there talking to the man who sold magazines. He had a few other things — combs, skin lotion, coinpurses. Suddenly Turner noticed the elephants and smiled. "No elephants, please!" But they were everywhere, all over the table. The child had been putting elephants between us, but suddenly he brushed them all into his hat. A waiter came with our steaming milk and the coffee grew hot again. In a while the other child, the son who'd been sent away, came back to his father's table. He'd been to the barber just around the corner; his hair was very short and it was slicked back with oil. The father smiled and thumped him on the back.

I want to remember those afternoons when we ate whatever we were served, and when Turner struck such a beautiful note with his spoon, and when I was still beautiful. Even the waiter with his large shoulders wore a white jacket, and the girl at the magazine stand stood looking at us.

We didn't take Socorro and Jesús out to dinner, but we invited them up to the apartment. There were three children, after all, and they weren't accustomed to going out. The shrimp had been lying in my bag all day but I got them out and boiled them; it was something I knew how to do. Jesús handled this food I had made as delicately as I handled the lettuce they brought upstairs with them. We were afraid of contaminating each other.

The children came in shyly, first Pepe, then Tomás. Jesús was holding the baby in his arms but after a while she fell asleep and we put her on my bed, under the eyes of the Virgin, buckling the shutters to keep her away from wind and charms. In the big room the older children cut pictures out of some old magazines. Of course I had no toys, but I had a little pair of nail scissors and plenty of *Newsweek*s and *Time*s. In one corner of the room, close to the kitchen, there was a stand-up bar made of bamboo. It was an ugly thing but Pepe brought their cut-out people over to it and made them talk while we drank beer and sat around the table.

I kept looking at Turner — at his hands, his white shirt, his face — seeing the children laugh, seeing Socorro's hair and her shoulders. It was strange to see Socorro with no work in her hands, nothing to hold now that the baby was asleep, nothing to grind or fry or boil or sweep. And it was strange to see Jesús sitting down, quiet in a chair with a bottle of beer. "Soon," Socorro told us, "is a good time to find *nopalitos*. Then I will fix them for you to eat. Delicious *nopalitos*."

Jesús said, "But without a car it's hard to get out to the hillsides. Also it's hard to cut the new growth off the old plant with a knife when you are there, and it's hard to peel the cactus when it is cut. We do this during La Semana Santa."

"We could go in Turner's car when it gets fixed," I said, translating all of this for him.

"Fifty dollars," Turner said. "That's what they told me at the place I went."

I translated. Turner tipped back in his chair. Jesús laughed when Socorro demonstrated the way to cut and peel *nopalitos*. "She's tough!" he said proudly.

Socorro raised her arm. "Sure, *hombre!* I had three brothers, didn't I? Didn't I climb trees and fight until I came to this town and had to behave like a lady! Believe me, I learned to defend myself from the cactus!"

Jesús had come from the pavement, where his mother raised him under a sheet of plastic spread on some poles and over a layer of newspapers spread on the ground. They'd slept in this makeshift house in separate commas of unconcern. But life under the sheet of plastic was simpler than life in the village his mother had left, because Jesús supported his mother and her other children as much as he could. He even bought them an egg now and then, since his own hens didn't lay enough for the needs of so many people. From her place on the sidewalk, Jesús' mother sold what she could. Once in a while she made the long trip back to her village and bought soft baskets to sell. They were popular with tourists. But unless she bought a lot of them, the cost of the trip ate up her profits. Also, there was no way of knowing how many baskets would be available. But this was part of her life of conjecture. Another part was begging, although the children did most of that. Jesús had shined shoes on the sidewalk and hired himself out for anything. By the time he was twelve, he made the trip to the village for the baskets and stayed with his grandfather, who had a goat and a cock and a blue house with a dog lying in the shade of a withered tree. His grandfather's sandals were the same color and texture as his feet. His grandfather's toenails were as hard and dark as wood. If the tree had worn clothes, the old man and his tree would have been indistinguishable. If he drank up the small profit of his maguey plant, who could blame him? He'd buried six daughters and one had moved to the city. He had only Jesús, his one useless grandson, to provoke him. Jesús told Turner all this while I translated. I could understand Spanish better now but I still couldn't speak it very well.

The baby woke up, and I went into my bedroom, where she was lying on the bed surrounded by pillows. She was only making small sounds and I didn't want Socorro to hear them, since she was sitting at the table with Jesús and Turner, so I closed the bedroom door and went over to the bed. I said, "*Cállate, shhh...*," and picked the baby up. She was heavy and wet. She smelled very interesting. I could feel my breasts, as if Turner had them in his mouth. Yes, I fed him so I would feed her. I pulled my blouse down, this peasant blouse embroidered in pink and red, made for this, and put my nipple into the baby's mouth. The baby began to suck. Her tongue cupped around my nipple, which touched the back of her throat.

"*No deje que le moleste*," I heard Socorro say, opening the door a crack. My back was turned. Do not hurt her? Or do not let her bother you? *Lo, le, la* the accusative tense. The baby's mouth was full of me. Before I turned around I put my hand up to my breast and the baby made a puckering sound as she released the round dark coin of my skin where everything goes out, everything is given, nothing is taken in. I handed her over. Socorro's blouse was wet.

"Sit here," I said. "And let me watch you feed her."

Socorro looked embarrassed. "They won't let you do this to yours," she said, but she opened her shirt, turning away slightly, and gave the baby her milk.

"Maybe I'll keep my baby."

Socorro was quiet for a minute. "Didn't you sign a paper with the señor?"

"Yes."

"You will owe him money now, if he's found a family for your baby. It will be very serious."

"How much?"

"Are you rich?"

"No."

"Then it isn't possible."

"If we get enough to pay for Turner's car, we can leave. Señor Hogan won't come after us."

Socorro said, "He won't forget. He is not always a good man."

"When you worked for him in his house? How long were you there?"

"It was two years."

"Was there ever a woman around?"

"Only us, the ones who worked for him."

"Did he make you...."

"Yes. But then Jesús came. That's why he sent me here. Because our men are not allowed in his house. He doesn't like men. He believes a woman should be pure. Like a nun. But once you are employed by the señor, you are with him for good."

I sat on the bed watching the baby suck.

"Take Elena now for a while. I'm going to sit with Jesús. Here. You look nice with her in your arms."

Motherlove, I thought, reaching out. What choice does a mother have, or her child? Does an infant wander the streets, go door to door examining faces for the one promising perfect maternal love? No, the baby takes what it gets and loves it, even the drinker, the abuser. What chance does the poor child have, or the mother? They are cut from the same bone. They're wrapped around each other. There is no boundary at all between them, no disgust. Where else does such acceptance occur? The interest in shit, the passing of food from one mouth to the other? The little belly? How it smells — or, better yet, the scalp. The pleasure of pushing your face down into it as the child curls and laughs and drools. Who else would you accept like this?

I held Socorro's baby and watched her fall asleep, tucked between my elbow and my breast. Children give power to mothers. But friends, lovers, fathers, contrive to take it away. As children, Kate and I slept in her twin beds as if we were sisters, one of us creeping across the narrow space between the beds to leap or crawl or slide into the arms of the other. I smelled her hair and breath. I was closer to her than her mother then. She would brush away her mother's hand, but not mine. Mine lay in hers or found its way to her cheek, her throat, her breasts with their flat nipples, and her stomach, also flat, like mine.

That night, after Jesús and Socorro and the children went down the stairs and into the place behind the wall, I lay on the table that was smeared with shrimp. It was a good height. I could wrap my feet around two of its metal legs and wrap my arms around Turner. It was the baby that excited me. Turner could put himself anywhere. He was already embedded in my flesh. I lay on my stomach and my body was wax. Turner could lift it, putting his hands under my stomach, which was full of life, pulling up on my bones and opening me. At first it was a surprise, but nothing is a surprise. We are born expecting everything. The long coil of juice I carried inside me made this sweet. I smelled of dark. I'd have made other places if I could for all this not asking, this not owning of myself.

The next morning I opened the glass and metal door to find a man standing on the landing. I was wearing the shirt that Turner had taken off. It was early. "I am wondering if I would find your friend here?" said the man. As if I had only one friend. In his dark suit and polished shoes, he eyed the table with its pile of shells suspiciously but he avoided my uncombed hair, my bare thighs. He held his breath as I held the door for him. In English he said, "Turner Hays. Is he here?" He was carrying a cane.

Turner came out of his room, rubbing the back of his neck. He had a towel wrapped around himself although he hadn't bathed. He edged over to our visitor and reached out a hand.

The man in black took a step back. He didn't know what to do with his eyes. Our apostasy was great but he was an uninvited guest. "This is Santos," Turner explained.

I tugged at the shirt and edged onto the sofa. "I could make some coffee, if we have any coffee. I could…"

"…go get dressed." Turner sat down and crossed his bare legs. "Something I can do for you?" he asked Santos.

The Cuban sat down on the wicker chair. "Well," he confided, casting a sidelong glance my way now that he was seated with another man, "yes, this is something." He tilted at me but I gazed at Turner, whose face was the field I had fallen into over and over during the night. And his hands, which were too small, which always surprised me.

"Another delivery?" Turner didn't smile.

"Picking up. Yes," Santos agreed.

"Something harmless? Groceries? Sure, that'd be great if I had a car and some time. But not what I did before. I'm definitely not the guy." His voice shook a little. "And I'd be interested to know what you're up to."

Santos sighed. "There are many children now leaving Cuba. Sent away even by their families. They go to Florida, of course, if they leave from the right place and can arrive in time."

"In time for what?"

"Nor to be eaten by a shark."

"That Yucatán baby wasn't Cuban, and I don't have a car."

"We provide the vehicle." Santos was staring at the floor. "Coming from Cuba. For children, it is a dangerous trip. There are so many who are not welcome there. We try to direct them to safety." He smiled. "So why not earn the money for your car, since it will not drive you home the way its condition is? We will pay for its repair and you will provide such service."

"This isn't about service! This is about you making money off of other people's troubles, Santos."

"You could be back in two days. Your car will be repaired by that time. Are you not going to work?" Santos looked grimly at me. "We could drink coffee," he went on, shifting his attention to Turner again, "if you were dressed in your clothes."

"Lily's going to loan me the cash," Turner replied. "I'm due back at school on Monday."

"But I don't have it, Turner."

Turner looked at me, pushed himself up, and retied the towel. We heard the click of the dog's claws on the floor in the bedroom. But we had bones in the refrigerator now.

This time Turner would drive to the coast alone, and he would take a truck that was blue and had the words *Para Siempre* painted in black over the windshield. It was the sort of truck you could carry large pieces of equipment on — as long as they weren't valuable, because it was an old truck. It was a Mexican truck, held together by stubbornness and powered by faith. It was hung with a crucifix and a dashboard Virgin and sixteen objects that were blessed or charmed. But without the requisite prayers, how would it ever get there and back? There were children who needed homes. Their parents were dead or in jail, but they had value and they had their own brief significance, Santos said. "Turner," he said. "You who are living here in the Apartamento de La Casa as a guest, why do you question to be a contributor?"

"The aparto.... Well hey, I'm Lily's guest. That's as far as I see it."

"You are a guest like the rest of us in this world. *Verdad?*"

He meant country, Turner thought, but he looked around the bar where they were drinking coffee and rum.

"Sunday you can return to a car that will be repaired. This is your investment. Also Señor Hogan will be indebted to you to such an extent that he will protect you from trouble about the other thing."

"What trouble? What're you talking about?"

"Only if there is any inquiring. There are so many legalities."

"What about cash?"

Santos told him. Two hundred. Turner managed to smile.

Four

✻

VERACRUZ IS A LARGE TOWN, a small city. It has energy and no real beauty. It lapses into the personal a few blocks from its *zócalo*. It likes the living and cares less for the dead than other parts of Mexico. It stretches along the water, enjoying itself, playing music down by the harbor and in the portales off the square. It likes to drink and it lowers the flag of Mexico with great ceremony every Monday afternoon, covering its fountain with a platform for the mayor and the military bands so that nothing will be dampened, not so much as a trombone.

In the daytime, the beach is dark and a little sticky. It isn't resort sand — it isn't white, it doesn't reflect the sun. Like a dark robe, it absorbs light. It absorbs everything. People wander up and down and dogs trot along sniffing at the sand as if they are looking for news. There are vendors on three-wheeled cycles with large carts between the front wheels. They sell soda pop and food and anything you can think of. Women carrying baskets call out. They have *tamales, tortillas, camarones;* everywhere there are baskets of small, boiled *camarones.* There will be a few slices of lime and some salt and something hot and red in a bottle. There are fruit-sellers with glass-covered carts — they carve the

mangoes fantastically and spear them on sticks. These too
come with salt and hot salsa. Everywhere on the daytime
beach people walk and eat and listen to the marimbas. Men
carry carved xylophones up and down the sand.

But at night the beach is bare. This is where Turner
pulled the truck off the road at last, rolled up the windows,
locked the doors, and fell asleep under a moon that rushed
in and out of the trees, hungry and thin. This is where the
dog lay on the floor of the cab and whined and where, at
three in the morning — the hour of terror — Turner woke
up sick as he'd never been sick before in his life. Was it
something he'd eaten? "Bad spirits," he kept muttering.
"Coming out of me, all this extremely bad shit." He
thought what he was about to do then must be wrong, for
he had superstitions even if he lacked beliefs. He found
himself saying things he didn't recognize. "I believe in one
holy catholicandapostolic," he said to the sand, because he
needed the certainty of words. It must have been a remnant
of his unbelievably short childhood, a time before his step-
father, when his mother still took him to church. Turner
was a dog in the sand. His head hung down between his
paws. His heart was turning on a spit, ripped from his chest,
a slice from throat to stomach exposed to the wind. He was
eviscerated. He knelt in the sand with his head down while
the other dog watched from the truck through the closed
window. Crying, he began to think of women, any woman.
He threw up and denied them. He was sorry he'd ever come
to rescue anyone and he was sorriest of all that he'd come to
rescue a bunch of children from the awful plank they rode
in the black three o'clock cold sea.

He would find them somewhere south of Boca del Río,
that's what Santos had said. Everything depended on it,

especially the children. If he could only get back in the truck and if the dog would only sit quiet and if his stomach would only sit quiet and if the truck would start. Nobody wanted kids. Not from Cuba, anyway. People might say so, but Turner didn't believe it any more than the mothers and older sisters who had given or sold or sent them away, and who had had nothing left but a little air in their stomachs and lungs with which to make this contract, one they had no doubt put off for as long as possible. A chance at survival and possibly something better! Who could say? Not Turner, whose stomach was a boat-sized knot. Doubled over, he hobbled back to the truck like a much older man, leaving pieces of himself all over the sandy soil of the Mexican highway, and he drove on to Boca del Río with the dog, such as he was, in order to meet the boat, such as it would be, at sunup. Unless there were winds, he thought bleakly. Unless the wind was against them. Failing that, the children would appear out of the dark water like angels on the head of a floating pin. Like butterflies impaled there, already damaged in transit.

The Cubans and their revolution. A man like Batista had governed by darkness. Alone. The king of casinos, drugs, whores. Castro had changed all that. So what was he doing here waiting for outcasts? At four a.m. Turner raised his head and saw the homeless children approaching in a fishing boat, its gunwales full of saltwater and weeds, its bow plunging down while the children, eight of them, wet and tired and hungry, came on to meet the day. He opened the door of the cab and got down carefully. They have names, he said to himself, feeling his swollen tongue fill his mouth and swallowing a new, bitter taste. He bent over. The smell of diesel fuel and oil had combined with the smell of wet weeds at his feet. He was going to be sick again; the fumes had invaded him and sweat came out on his face and throat like a warning before he threw up the last bile his stomach owned, a pale yellow string of it, and his ass burned and stung like the ass of a man violated for the first time.

Afterwards he tried to walk far enough to get down to the edge of land the wretched pin with all its victims was approaching. Jesus. They couldn't feel as rotten as he felt. He made his way slowly. A man hunched at the wheel of the boat glared at him from the sea. The men took each other's measure; Turner was hunched over too. One needed a shave as much as the other — their chins bristled with a matching fury of whiskers. Turner had another sack in his hand, this one fatter than the last and made of plastic.

Then there was sudden quiet as the man in the boat cut the engine and the children, the small hopes of a very small country, looked out at the endless coastline in front of them.

Turner waded into the oily, bone-strewn, fouled-up water, rocks underfoot, the boat rocking too, spilling out kids now like a tired untied shoe, a bad nursery rhyme that hurt his mind. The kids...they were cringing.... One of them was even curled up under the cockpit, trying to hide. Could he look worse than the man at the wheel?

"*Sonospolasuel?*" the man said indifferently.

Turner shook his head and shrugged. "*Sí.*" All of it was gibberish. This was only worse.

"*Oco.*" It was a lisp or maybe it was Cuban or something else. The man was missing several teeth.

Turner held up eight fingers and nodded, his mouth as dry as the vulture that sat on a thatched roof a little way down the beach. The plastic sack dangled from his right thumb, which was curled against his palm. He threw it into the boat. Then he put out his hands for the children, who were passed down to him one by one, children who looked like they'd been picked out of motherless alleys, tiny children holding tinier ones. Brothers and sisters themselves holding infants in their skinny arms.

In a matter of minutes the captain, or the one who'd got the boat this far, was peeling the last child — the one wedged into the small space under the cockpit — off the surface of the slimy wood and delivering him to Turner's hands, handing him down into the mess of sea like a thing pulled out of a shell, something edible, not to be wasted.

Turner lined the children up on the cold morning sand, still holding the curled one in his arms, and turned to see whether the boat would pull away or anchor itself. *"Hasta luego,"* he called tentatively, straightening himself up. But the man in the boat didn't answer and the boat rode the water, plunging and rising indecisively. When Turner turned his back on it one of the little boys was crawling away, his four thin limbs pawing out of the muck at the edge of the sea toward higher ground, scrabbling fast out of reach. Turner deposited the curled-up one in a hole in the rough sand. "Stay," he said to the children and babies, with all the authority he could find in himself. Still damp from the retracted tide, the incline was slippery. Eight. I'm supposed to get eight. "Stay! I mean it!"

Ahead, two boys had appeared from nowhere and they were circling a shadow only one shade more solid than the land. "Hey! You leave him alone!" Turner shouted, suddenly afraid for the runaway boy. "You hear? Get off! Get away now!" There was a kicking, rolling creature moving under the silence of a tall, parched tree. Six arms. Six legs. "Get off! *Vete! Vete!*" Turner reached in and pulled at arms, hair, yanking at whatever came to hand, some shiny cloth, some skin, a bare, filthy foot, the toe like a small root, like something unused to light. One of these children was his; one of them had come in on the boat and he was responsible. Where had the others come from? He pulled the smallest of the three out of the pile of skin and bones and cloth, grabbing a foot, an extremity, the kid screaming, the leg bent the wrong way, the face, under everything, filthy — dirt coming through the teeth like meal, like something taken in on purpose, and the nose smudged in snot and blood. "Hey, it's okay." He gathered the boy to his own shirt. But did he have the right one? Did it matter? Who was going to speak up if he carried the wrong one back to the truck and drove away? The other two boys moved off as if they had never seen each other before, as if they'd been possessed by something alien to both of them, a piece of flesh on an empty beach. One of them was limping. But this leg that was draped over his arms had to be broken, or anyway it was pulled way out of line. It hung down like something defeated. This face...when did I even touch a little kid? Turner thought. Years. Probably myself only ten. But it feels weird, this skin so weightless on my own, and all this grief not mine, not even a woman's.

He stumbled back to the children squatting on the sand. The wet one was still lying in the hole, a little chin tucked in, a little nipple sticking to the clothes, Christ, the wet one's another girl, Turner thought, surprised that it made any difference to him. But she was older, maybe eleven or twelve, and she had cut her hair and dressed like a boy. "Okay kids! *Niños!* Vamoose! Let's get on out of here." The words he used were as unfamiliar as the voice, but little by little the children hobbled to the big truck sloped against the trees, leaning slantwise at the tip of the grimy road. Turner packed two girls holding babies in the filthy cab where the dog sat waiting. No more were ever going to fit. They were going to have to ride on the back. He led them around to the platform. "You have to sit, hear? No standing up!" He climbed up to demonstrate, feeling a return of energy when he balanced dangerously on the edge of the platform and looked down at their sleepy faces. Then he sat down, thinking he was not a bad person, really, but what did he know about kids? Most of the time he didn't even think about them. There were four on the flatbed. Four there and four up front. He was going to be counting all day. He was going to be driving at a snail's pace, he could see that, with no way to bolt the kids down. He gave the boy with the hurt leg a soft push and laid him down on the flatbed with both hands, moving him over to the center for safety.

The dog was underfoot, next to the gearshift when Turner started the truck. He yanked at the gears and the truck lurched forward, jolting, and something hit the dust behind. Turner heard a thud and closed his eyes. He was sore, his head ached like a wound, but he pushed the door open and leaned out, draping himself almost to the road, where he saw the boy with the leg, who'd fallen off head first.

He'll have to come up here, Turner thought, or maybe he said this out loud to the girls and the babies but they didn't understand. One of the babies began to cry. Turner climbed down, almost falling, feeling his legs buckle as they hit the ground. The kid in the road hadn't moved, so he went over,

because the leg really did look twisted up, and then he had
to get down on his knees and angle the kid against his chest
so he could raise himself and the boy back up. It was easy
opening the door of the truck with his right hand, but
shooing the kids in the cab out while he laid this one down
was rough. The girls argued and cursed. But they climbed
down and pulled the little ones out and stood sullenly in the
dust. Turner went around back. "Now sit like I said to, like
I told you. Hold on to these stakes, and make room for
these girls. Here, look how I'm showing you. This is a life-
and-death thing." He wrapped one of the children's arms
around a stake that poked up out of the flatbed of the truck.
The bend of a child's arm, like a thin river wrapping around
an improbable tree.

He looked at his work. It would be better to tie them.
But how? Not with the sad, stinking clothes they wore on
those bone-puny bodies. Not with the weeds next to the
truck that rip like weeds will rip. Not with the handkerchief
he'd lost a while back. The dog rope, that would do for one
of them. Or even two. And the towel he hid after he threw
up — it could save a life. He went to the cab of the truck
and took the rope off the dog's throat and pulled the towel
from the place he'd stowed it behind the seat. "Now then.
There you go! *Nombres?*" he said, approaching the smallest
two boys and wrapping the dog rope around one waist and
then the other in a figure eight.

"Paco."

"Jaime."

"Good. Now guys, you sit down tight and remember
what I said about holding on." Turner wanted them to
understand. He genuinely did. Now for the towel. He
picked the eleven-year-old girl for this indignity, and tied

her to the firmest stake, slipping his hand between the knot and her shirt to make sure it wasn't tight. She'd been afraid of getting raped by that dude on the boat, no doubt; her eyes had gone as blank as pigeon eyes. *"Nombre?"*

"Paco."

"Sure, darling. Only we can't have two Pacos. I'd never get through the day."

She spoke with a voice almost not heard. "Paco."

"Bueno. What's another Paco more or less?" Turner peeled his blue shirt off without unbuttoning it. "Who's next?" The two girls with the babies in their arms were still untied, looking up at him. One bit her lip nervously. "Okay, that's it. *Nombre?"*

"María."

"Other side. Like on the boat. Can't have the *Para Siempre* flipping over, can we? The Forever truck on the long road to the House of Happiness. Got to keep the total harmonious death-defying equilibrium. Centripetal orbiters, that's what we are. Squatters on the nirvana truck. I bet you guys are getting a little interested in some breakfast, right? The word of truth on the road to happiness. Well, I'm going to find it for you once we get this act in gear." Turner ripped the blue shirt in half as he talked and pulled the sleeves off. "Okay, María, here you go." He used half the shirt, choosing a sleeve and tying it to her wrist and to the baby's wrist. *"Nombre?"*

"Juana."

"Good girl. Sit down here, Juana. Have a seat. Next to María and all is well. This your little brother? You get the whole rest of my shirt, see? The shirt right off my back, and that must be brotherliness if I ever heard of it. So let's get going and get some food into our emptiness, whatta you say? One more. *Nombre?*"

"Fidel."

"I'll bet you are." Turner noticed a small note pinned to
Fidel. He pulled it off and read: *Fidel Morelos. Hasta mis
padres me buscan, por favor.* He climbed back in the truck's
cab. He was shivering. He put the injured boy's head on his
lap. *"Nombre?"*

"Carl."

"Carlos? Good for you, kiddo."

"Carl. I America."

"How'd you get to be America, Carl?"

"Father. Him America."

"Right." It didn't seem wise to go into town. Veracruz
would be humming by now and the truck looked a little
strange, to say the least. It looked like the work of the devil.
Para Siempre — Turner hoped so. He hoped it would make
it back to the orphanage, even if not for always. The *"para"*
is directional. Toward eternity.

Turner drove as if there were a frame around them and
the children couldn't spill out of it, because otherwise he
couldn't drive at all. He drove as if they were all going to be
all right. He drove slowly, although they were all hungry as
with one stomach and some of them leaked into their
clothes and the road turned whimsically and climbed
unsteadily as if it had no end in mind for them.

After a while he pulled over. There was a truckstop at the
side of the highway, an affair of sticks and tin that ran along
for almost half a block and had bags of dried fruit and
coconut and bananas tied onto its rafters. There was a little
table and three chairs, some radio music, a refrigerator, a
girl in a pink dress with a runny nose, a woman, a place to
fry the roadside food that men in trucks came here to buy.

Turner parked the truck so that the back of it, with the children tied to it, was out of sight. He couldn't possibly undo all the ropes and knots. He figured the señora wouldn't look around, she'd just fry up some *tortillas* for the kids and take his pesos. He'd get a bunch of Coca-Colas too, to wet the throats that had been salted in a sea of tears.

Not a sound from in back as he climbed out. Maybe they all went to sleep, Turner thought. Maybe they were tired out from that boat and the perfectly understandable feelings that accompany sendoffs, goodbyes — hell, who'd they say goodbye to, he wondered. Then he wondered if he should get the señora to take a look at the injury to that boy's leg. Carl's. The leg didn't look good at all. But then again, what if something was seriously wrong? A woman like that could do him more harm than good in that case.

"Carl, wake up, here's some chow." Turner was back at the truck window with a paper plate. "Come on, here you go." Suddenly he saw one of the boys running back to the truckstop with his hand out, yelling. *"Señora, dame una tortilla? Por favor señora!"*

"Por favor señora!" Another one had escaped. They'd come untied and leapt off the truck like rabbits toward some leafier place, where the woman under the tin roof was still frying the *tortillas* he'd ordered. *"Dame!"* Give. Give. *"Dame! Por favor...."*

Shit. It was more than he was good for, all the chasing that was required. He was defeated by a bunch of refugees he was breaking his back to save. What the hell. He pulled the truck up a few hundred feet and set off into a field of fruit trees and bare ground, and the children followed him a few minutes later with their warm *tortillas* full of beans,

and Carl stayed put in the truck while everybody else, even
the dog, lay around on the ground, chewing and looking up
at the sky, which was empty overhead.

When Turner opened his eyes the children were sitting
around him in a circle. The dog was under a different tree,
in a different shade all his own. For a minute Turner wondered if the children were thinking about killing him so
they could escape, maybe thinking about pounding him to
death with the rocks that lay around the trunks of the fruit
trees. The sun was high in the sky already. He was hot. He
wanted a beer. His stomach hurt — he shouldn't have eaten
the beans. It was time to get back on the truck, but first he'd
walk back to the *fonda*, get a little life in his legs, get a beer
and some clean water for the dog.

"Agua, señora? Por favor? Por el perro." The woman in the
fonda stood by her stove and looked at him. She served men
all day long, from early morning until night, but she would-
n't serve Turner again — not with those children who
weren't his riding the bare back of that truck. She looked at
him and pointed to a blue plastic bowl that sat on the table.
The little girl with the runny nose had disappeared. She was
asleep somewhere behind something; she couldn't have
wandered very far, not on this highway. He reached for the
bright blue plastic bowl. Then he thought the woman
wouldn't want the dog to drink out of it because she used it
on the table, for food, for the men she served all day.
"Agua," Turner said again, *"por el perro."*

She stood staring at him.

There was a container over in the corner, a clay jug with
a dish on top to keep dirt and bugs out. Turner picked up
the bowl and walked to the back of the stall and used the
wooden dipper that lay next to the jug to splash water into

the bowl, which grew heavier in his hand, and carried it carefully back to the dog, setting it down on the cement floor of the *fonda,* the shelter leaning so diligently away from the highway and the sun. The full bowl looked clean and inviting on the cement, the way a new bowl of water always looks, and the dog leaned down to it immediately.

"Mister mister!" One of the little boys was flying up the edge of the field, wings spread, mouth open. "Mister!" Turner looked at the señora. Their eyes met. Then he turned and ran. He moved fast. The dog was following, trotting along. "Him bad. Mister."

Turner reached the vehicle and yanked the door open. Carl, the little boy with the injured leg and the injured face, was gray. His mouth was open like the mouth of a caught fish, bubbling. And the leg looked terrible, as if it had been brought there for someone else and left in the wrong place. *"Vete a la señora!"* Could you die from a leg? The woman was running at them now, the only thing anywhere with direction. Her shoes slapped the path between the little *fonda* and the highway where the truck sat at the edge, hot and hard as a pan on a fire, warming up minute by minute. Slap slap slap, she ran. She pushed past him and bent inside the dark body of the cab to look at the boy. She began talking in a steady stream of words, quick commands to the children. She sent some of them back for water and rags and a broom. She spoke to the boy firmly, asking him questions. When the children got back to the truck, she grabbed the broom and raised it above her head as if she would punish all of them at once, but she brought it down with a great crack over the edge of the truck door, on the passenger side next to Carl who lay with his leg partly thrust out into the morning. She unbuttoned his cotton pants and pulled them down over his hips while his mouth made fish noises in the air, and she told a child to go back to the *fonda* and bring the blue water bowl and wet Carl's face and give him a drink. And while he drank, the woman ran her hand over the leg and around it, her palm and fingers almost circling the thigh, and suddenly pulled down on it and pushed it the other way. A howl went up from inside the cab.

Turner watched the woman wipe her hands on the apron, lift it, and take it off. He watched her wipe her eyes with it and then wrap it thoughtfully around the broken stalk of the broom, binding it to the broken leg. But when she straightened, she turned on him and leveled her eyes at his and pulled her lips back. A jet of spittle flew out of her mouth and fell in the dirt. *Pffh!* She slid away backwards like something hurrying out of a fouled place, and she made the sign of the cross over her breast as she left with her head bent, her body heavy on the footpath, not slapping but silent, so that it was the earth that rocked back and forth underneath.

Clouds gathered over the fruit trees in the field while Turner tied the children to the staves of the truck and got in and drove on to the town that lay in the bowl of the mountains, the truck lurching and coughing and sending fumes over the children who were bound to it for safekeeping.

Five

PALM SUNDAY. I WAS ALONE. But the streets were full of people going to church and bringing something to be blessed — a picture of the Virgin, a cross of woven palms. Things that would fend off evil spirits in the days ahead. Earlier that day I had been down to Socorro's again.

"*Mira*. I cannot give you lessons any more. I am very sorry," Socorro said sadly.

"Because of Señor Hogan? He told you that? He told me too. Why do we have to pay attention to him?"

She nodded and shrugged, then she opened the door and I sat on the striped sofa in her everything room and watched her working on a giant figure made out of cloth, paper mâché, and paint. He had a big nose and a big penis sticking out of his pants. "What is it?"

"Judas!" She sounded surprised. *"Por la semana santa."*

"He's very ugly, Socorro!"

"Never mind. In a few days he will go to jail, and we will burn him in a fire."

I started to tell her about the trip Turner had been hired to make but she said, "It is better not to tell me. And for him it is better not to do this. He is Americano."

"So is the señor."

"But he has important friends here."

I considered this. I watched an egg being cracked; I watched a child being scolded and put outside the shelter of the room. Then clothes were gathered for a wash. Socorro wouldn't let me help. "No," she said, grabbing things. I knew she'd wait until I left, then go to the place where the neighborhood women met to do their washing. It had several ribbed concrete sinks. The water was always cold, but the labor of rubbing the clothes against the surface, which was as smooth as soapstone except for the ribs, made up for the lack of heat. Then there was the sun, which whitened. Each woman carried the wet things home in a basket, either on her head or on her hip, and in each yard there were lines or bushes or the backs of chairs and in each kitchen there were places for the wet clothes to hang during rainy weather. "We could use the hot water in my kitchen."

"But how would they be clean then, without the rubbing?" she wanted to know.

Besides which, I thought, she wouldn't want to do the washing in my presence, and she would miss the company of her friends. "But some of those are my clothes," I pointed out. "You don't have to do my laundry just because Señor Hogan says so. I could do my own if you'd show me how."

"It would make the other women too nervous."

In spite of her politeness, I felt hurt. She must have seen that because she said, "How is that little boy?"

"Which one?"

"The one without words. The corn child."

"Why do you call him that? He isn't running away."

She didn't answer, but went on gathering clothes, moving around the room nervously. I said, "I should not come to your house any more, should I? Even as a friend."

Socorro looked down. I felt very sad just then, for both of us.

"It doesn't matter," I said. "I'm going to leave here soon anyway."

"How will you get away? What about the señor?"

"I'm going to play a trick on him."

"What will you do?"

"I'll tell him I lost the baby."

"You can go home. You can have the baby. But don't tell the señor anything. He will be very mad because of the money."

"Socorro, you shouldn't be afraid of him."

"But he will move me again. This time to something bad."

"Like what?"

"He says he has a place in another town where women have to do things with men. My husband would be ashamed. And my children. He would take me from them."

"Socorro, that can't be true! He can't make you do something like that."

She didn't say anything. Then she said, "*No comprendes.*" You do not understand.

"Does he pay you for taking care of this place?"

"*Qué dice?*" Socorro put her hand over her mouth, as if she thought the idea was strange. "We are getting our house here, aren't we?" she said.

"I'm going to tell Turner everything, Socorro. I'm going home with him. When Mr. Hogan comes looking for me, tell him you saw me when you were making the Judas."

Socorro smiled. "Like the corn child?"

I stood up and looked around her everything room for

the last time. "You will miss the little *nopales*," she said. "How sad it will be."

I got some money out of my pocket and put it on her table. I was kept by Mr. Hogan too, after all. Then I went up the metal stairs and lay on my bed. I put my hand up in the dark to feel the baby's dimpled leg. When I am a mother I'll look in my child's face every day for the first signs of abandonment, I thought. Parents raising children, pouring so much of themselves away in the process, and then? For the child everything changes. Chairs doorways clothes growing bigger or smaller. And the child doesn't even remember the half-hour spent in her mother's arms during a thunderstorm. But the mother remembers as if it were yesterday. She can feel the bones of the child's back, the knees, the hollows behind them. She can feel the weight of the child, and remember when she reached down and knew she couldn't lift the child any more because the child was just then, at that moment, grown too heavy. The mother saves the drawings made by the child, and the things made out of paper and glue, and the pincushion that has some lace around its edge. Each of these things is an icon in the house the mother has shared with the child, who grows embarrassed and forgets with what pride the drawing or carved cat was presented in the first place. Each gift was presented as if the mother was a lover. And they were, once upon a time, in love, the child and the mother. It was mutual. Then the mother becomes something else — a slight obstacle to other loves. The mother clings to hallways airports telephones and her child's busy life. But the child is always going. The mother is always waiting for a visit, but it is only a visit. The child doesn't even unpack. There is a bag sitting on the floor of the child's room and it is full of clothes and some things the mother doesn't remember. She doesn't think she chose those things. The mother is necessary now in small ways, but for her nothing has changed except this. She still feels the weight of the head on her breast, the hollows of the legs behind the knees. She still wakes with a start at four in the morning over something in the child's life.

I wondered where all the mothers of the children were — the children in my room at La Casa Feliz.

On Monday I went back to school. Señora Hidalgo told me Mr. Hogan was expecting some new children to arrive any minute, but of course I knew that already. I knew what Turner was doing. And I knew he was late.

I only had six students now, so Señora Hidalgo thought it would be possible for me to take three or four of the ones who were coming, although the truth was that Alexander and the others required all of my attention. I tried to explain this but it didn't do any good and it didn't matter anyway. I was ony thinking of Turner. I was thinking about how to tell him the truth. It was part of him too, the thing that was growing inside me.

In the middle of the morning I was called out of the classroom by Señora Hidalgo. She had the girl named Carmen with her — the one who took care of the children at night. They stood in the corridor and Señora Hidalgo was even holding a corner of Carmen's sweater, as if she feared that she might escape. "The señor is going to see you," she announced, leaving Carmen in charge of my classroom. Then she followed me up the corridor, as if my escape was also a possibility. "Go on," she said, behind me.

I was walking like my grandmother. Toe heel toe heel, as if silence mattered here, as if we were still an order of nuns. I straightened my dress, brushing my palm over it and tugging as well.

Mr. Hogan sat at the same desk, although it looked smaller now. It looked inadequate in its effort to cover him. We were alone except for Señora Hidalgo, who was rummaging around within hearing distance. I had things to say to him but he spoke up first. "Apparently your boyfriend is on his way back," he said. "Which should please you. And if all goes well, he'll make enough money to go away, which pleases me. He'll have money tonight. Since he seems to have a flair for this kind of thing, I'm going to ask him to take one of the children up to the States when he goes back. We have a placement in Texas."

I wanted to tell him my decision, but how could I tell him I wanted to keep my baby when Turner didn't even know about it yet? I glanced at Mr. Hogan, who was gazing up at me "...these kids," he was saying, "...they don't have ID in the legal sense, so the border can be tricky." He thought for a minute. "We arrange papers for immigration to make things easier."

"What papers?"

Mr. Hogan pushed his chair back and stood up. "The boy will have to cross as Turner's child, that's all."

"He can't do it alone," I said.

"What? Be a father?" Mr. Hogan laughed.

I decided to bargain. If Turner gets back in the next hour, Kate can have him. There's still time enough for him to get back to school.... If not.... I looked at the clock and thought of rolling away from everything. Mr. Hogan and I were face to face. "He won't do it," I said. Mr. Hogan trailed his fingers across the desk and cleared his throat. "There are things that can get misunderstood. Your situation here — do you want your friends and family to find out? I told you, the work I'm doing down here is delicate. You're part of my faculty. I wish you'd remember that."

"We're all pregnant, Mr. Hogan! Your faculty! We're all having babies that are illegitimate."

"The fact is, I'm sheltering you girls and some homeless children from the world." He bent over and picked something up from the floor. A pin. When he straightened, we were eye to eye.

"What time do you think he's getting back?" I said, trying to hold myself still.

Mr. Hogan looked at his watch. "That's one thing I don't control."

An hour passed and then another. We were waiting, Señora Hidalgo and I. Sooner or later Turner would arrive at the fields outside of town and lower himself into them, like someone sore from a long battle. The little town spread out its arms and neighborhoods, all those small industries on its outer edges and the repair shops where everything was fixed again and again. Nothing is ever wasted in Mexico. There is another life in every death, and death is small. It is an adversary, nothing more.

"I wonder at what hour they are coming," Señora Hidalgo said once or twice, glancing at her wrist to check the dial of a small expansion-bracelet watch. Her heels tapped the tiles. Even her fingernails clicked, touching this or that on her desk, straightening papers and lining up the blue-and-gold ballpoint pen and the ceramic lady with wide skirts that hid her paperclips. "That truck was ridiculous.

We should not have sent your friend in that truck. And your friend? Will he be entirely...." She paused. "Have we expected too much? He has not even been in this country. How long is it? It makes only a short time since this friend of yourself has arrived and we send him across the mountains with a very old truck to receive a cargo of children. *Pobrecitos.* How could he ever manage this? And if he does not, what will the consequence be?"

"You're worried."

"Of course, not for myself at all. It is for the little ones. And perhaps even for your friend I am worried if you say to me that I should be." Tap tap. The window was blank, but the air outside was thickening. Then rain began to fall, quick and violent. In moments, a skyful hit the ground outside. Señora Hidalgo coughed. "This wet road is very bad for the truck," she said. "It will never get through now."

"All of us together could put some rocks in the holes."

"Don't be crazy!" she said loudly. "The rain stops every day and then we would have stones in our road and no one could pass over them."

"When it stops, we'll move the stones," I said impatiently.

Señora Hidalgo said, "If we don't put the stones out we don't have to take them away again." Then she added reasonably, "*Mira*, Carmen brought the children downstairs. Although it is late, they are in your classroom. It will take your mind away from worrying if you go to them."

So I went into my classroom with its miniature chairs and faces. The girl named Carmen was there, her hair pulled back in several places and one button of her dress undone. It was raining hard and all the windows were dark. There was water running down the long spout outside, water from the roof tiles overhead. It hit the courtyard in splashes and ran down the unpaved lane. Beyond this there was the muddy road. "Hello," I said in English, and the six remaining children chanted, "Good morning, teacher."

"It's raining," I said.

They looked at me blankly. "*Lluvia*," I said, pointing at the wall of windows, while Carmen in her unbuttoned dress stood there stupidly, her feet crossed, her arms dangling.

Diego said, "*Sí*." Juana said, "*Sí*," huskily. Alexander said nothing. He was in his usual crumpled position, looking at the area around his bare feet. The sound of the rain was like drums.

"Alexander?" I said. The child started slightly, then slumped over again in the plastic chair. "Alexander, are you fine today?"

He put his head down on the table and turned it away.

"I cannot hear you Alexander. *Cómo estás?* Come here. *Ven aqui*." The Spanish was so much kinder, with its familiar. "We are going outside to put rocks in the road. *A poner piedras! Ven aqui*."

Suddenly we heard the sound of a horn. A long blast! Señora Hidalgo rushed down the hall and out into the heavy rain and we followed, the children tumbling out of the convent, passing us and running on to the end of the muddy lane. The truck was stuck there, its wheels embedded in the ground.

When Turner pushed the truck door open he looked wilder than ever. His hair sprang out from his scalp and his lips were drawn back, but I ran at him and held him in the waterfall of rain. I pressed him against me and he pressed back. Señora Hidalgo saw the children on the flat, worn bed of the truck, shattered by streams of water as thick as arms around them. She reached out but they were fastened to the truck, so she began to unwrap and untie them and to chafe their skinny bodies with her hands. *"Adentro!"* she told them, still unwrapping, promising them all kinds of things if only they would come undone and run inside: warm chocolate and candy and beds, although none of these things existed in that place.

Turner wiped his face with the back of his arm and shook himself. "What day is it?" he gasped. "It's Monday, right? The car should be ready. Yes?"

"Yes."

His arm was around my waist. "Then let's get out of here. I never want to see this place again. Is Hogan in there? I'm going to hang him by his balls."

"It's late. He's gone home."

"He owes me money."

"He said you'd get it tonight."

"And my car too?"

"I think so. You can get it in the morning. Is it big enough for both of us?"

"You mean you're coming with me?"

"Yes!"

We heard Señora Hidalgo shouting. Where was the eighth little boy, she wanted to know, rushing back to the truck in the rain. Turner opened the cab again to let the dog jump out. The eighth little boy? He pointed at something lying damply on the plastic-covered seat, burning in fever on a broomstick. The boy who was so much a part of him now that he'd forgotten him.

"Madre!" Señora Hidalgo's hands flew to her face. *"Adentro!"*

So Turner lifted the wounded child out of the truck, his sweaty cheeks and eyelids catching the rain as it plunged down, and we trailed carefully behind. The wet, limp child was held against Turner, across his arms, head back, his streaming hair marking a trail through the dark hall of La Casa Feliz.

That evening I said at last, "Turner, I need your help." I was walking beside him. I was moving my legs and mouth. "Because I'm going to have a baby," I said. We were walking on the street outside the compound.

"Lil, don't fool around. I've only been here a week." This was Turner's way of trying to joke.

"Don't you remember?" I put my hand on his arm.

Suddenly he understood. "That's impossible. Lil! Please."

We had reached the arch. I touched it as we passed. "It's been since January. This is March." We crossed the street. We seemed to have nowhere to sit. We walked and walked around the block, where Mr. Hogan's compound rose up beside, behind, beside us.

"Why didn't you say something before?"

"I didn't know I wanted it until now. Until you came. Turner, this is your baby too," I said. "But if you reject it, it'll be Gus Hogan's."

"What do you mean by that?"

"I mean I signed some papers. To get the baby adopted."

"Get an abortion, for Christ's sake! That makes more sense. Down here you can get one in the blink of an eye."

"Couldn't you want it?"

"Not after what I just did," he said, as if our child would arrive by boat. "No thanks, Lil," as if I were selling something at the door. "No thanks," he said again. His voice was trembling. There, in the center of the compound, were Socorro and Jesús and their children. A dog was barking. Our dog was following, sniffing at posts and trees and curbs. Turner was spilling out words now: "It was just…I only came down here because…." I don't remember all of them, but they are still written on my body. The marks of no and no and because.

I said, "I'll keep it then. I can do it alone." But I was moved by Turner's fear. More than anything, I was moved by the fact that he'd shown it to me.

"Here? Without any friends or family! Are you crazy? That's insane. You'll ruin your life. And mine. And what about Kate? Don't you care about her?" That was terrible, but he didn't stop. "What's more important, her happiness or that little bit of nothing inside you? Get rid of it, Lily. Otherwise you'll break her heart."

It was true that people came to Mexico to get rid of babies. And it was true that the child was nothing yet, only a small thing lying inside me. But the thought of digging it out…. We kept walking. Turner's boots were as silent as skin, so that only his shape marked the movement next to me, his swaying as he met the surface of the earth with his stubborn limp.

"What if we stayed down here?"

"What for, Lily? There's nothing here for me. And I want to go back to school. I'm on probation. I'll get drafted if I don't make it back."

"Then I'm going with you."

"Not now, you're not. Not to have that baby."

"Because of Kate?"

"If that makes it easier."

But after the party, when Kate took off her clothes and put her body against his, day after day, and I had to share the same room with them, wasn't he already part of my flesh. "I didn't expect you to come," I said. "But now that you have, I know what I want." I took his hand and looked at his face, hoping for a change of heart. A declaration. But nothing happened. The moon was beginning to burn through the cloth sky. It was brighter all the time, and the air was soft. As if I had grown a new piece of intelligence, something extra, I listened to Turner and heard what he thought. It was like being able to see in the dark.

"Lil, I'm sorry. But I didn't ask to sleep with you that night. This is no time to be having babies, Lil. Not for either of us. Look at the state of the world!"

I went upstairs. The smell of rain blew in from the open door. In a while Turner came up and crawled onto the mattress and I turned out the lights. I didn't want Mr. Hogan to come, because Turner would leave when he got paid. Kate wasn't the problem any more. I wanted this man more than I wanted my friend. I wanted him more than I wanted my own flesh and blood.

"Turner," I whispered. "All right. If you'll take me with you, I'll do what you want."

Remember me then. In the arms of this man. And remember me an hour later, sitting alone when Turner got up to let my employer in. The man who housed me. The man who still owned my child. I could hear them talking, giving and receiving money. Pesos. "I wanted it in American," I heard Turner say. "I don't even know how much this is."

He'll take the money, though, I thought from my position on his bed. And he'll go back to school and to Kate, who is waiting to lie down with him again. Unless I do what I said.

Then Turner said, "Wait, this is only half."

"The rest will be at the border," Gus Hogan said. "I thought Lily would have told you about my offer."

"Well, she didn't. And how do I get my car? I need the cash for it, man." The voice leaving Turner's throat was furious. "Listen, this is payment for something I already did! I want the money. I worked for it." There was not much air around the words.

"In addition to the balance, I can offer you a generous bonus."

"If I do what this time?"

"Take a little boy up to the border."

"There's something wrong with all this, Hogan."

"That's a matter of interpretation. We're trying to help kids and we have to contend with laws that aren't always reasonable. Look at those Cuban kids. They're desperate."

Then I heard a strange sound. I sat in the dark and listened so hard that I decided I was hearing Turner's heart beating through the wall. Finally Mr. Hogan said, "I can give you papers that will get you both across. This is one of Lily's boys. He's a difficult case. You'd be doing him a favor. There aren't many chances for a boy like him."

Alexander.

"What kind of papers?"

"You'll have a false name. And he'll have the same one."

"You mean you'd make him look like he's my kid?"

"That's right."

"Wouldn't it be easier if he had two parents?"

I took a deep breath.

"You mean Lily? She and I have a previous arrangement."

"Not any more, you don't."

"Our arrangement is quite mutual."

"I doubt it. She's not having the baby. She got rid of it."

Silence. Then, "Somebody local? Gomez again?"

Turner said, "I'll take the poor kid up, I don't care. But get me two sets of papers and my car. And wipe out whatever so-called debt Lily has for this place you put her in." I heard the front door opening. "And I want two hundred dollars at the border." The door slammed shut.

Then it was the next day, the last day, and I was lying in a room where a different thing happens than love, the opposite thing, but similar because I was lying on my back, my knees apart, a man there, in almost the same way. Downstairs there was a courtyard where musicians came to sing their songs in the evenings. A restaurant, a bar, two or three cafés. This was the corner of town where we were entertained. Mariachis were hired by couples. They were like teams, vying with each other for the finest chords. The couples hired these champions of love, and later they went into one of the restaurants for beer or tequila or rum. Turner and I had come here once or twice, but now it was the place to have the seed of us unjoined.

"Be still," the man named Gomez said in broken English. "Or it is pain like hell."

Pain. There was no antidote. It was better to be awake, to experience this death, and if I moved it would have killed me too, the sharp instrument. At that moment, lying there looking at nothing on his ceiling, I didn't care. There was a long, ugly crack over me that matched my own. My legs stretched across the room, across the town, from one side of it to the other, they were strapped so far apart, and there was still real life inside me, a future, a real infant.

At that moment, I would rather have killed myself than kill this child. I told myself that there would be a reprieve, that someone would rush in, Turner would change his mind. Or that Kate would arrive — she'd always rescued me.

Time. He was standing there with the metal in his gloved hands. "Close your eyes and bite down on the towel, please."

It would have entailed a scene, such explanations, to get up and walk away. I could hear cars, children, even a horse outside. There was the sound of a tiny boat fired by a candle, jetting around in a pail of water, a harmless toy being sold on the street under the window. I could imagine the rest, the town filled with houses, with mothers and fathers, with children crying and sleeping and playing and babies pulling at breasts. "Hold still, señorita."

The pain was unendurable. My own knife had turned against my heart. Heaven. Hell. In that order. After death, judgment.

I took a taxi back to Calle de los Arcos and knocked on the heavy door that was part of the courtyard wall. I couldn't go up the stairs — they seemed too steep. The door opened to reveal the everything room where Socorro and Jesús had offered the valuable chicken to the ground before the cement was poured, and where the sofa was covered in stripes and children. Two boys.

Jesús handed me some paper flowers, I don't know why, I didn't ask — blue for love, red for life. Of course I shook the hand he offered me. I glanced around. "Socorro? *Dónde está?*" There was the ceiling with its wooden beams, its hanging ears of corn and bags of chickenfeed, a crucifix and the familiar saints, the stove where Socorro had brought forth miracles, the cold cement in front of it, the water jar with its dish, and the table with its oilcloth, the walls. But Socorro was not there.

The children ran out to the patch of ground where the chickens were squatting silently, and where the fronds of a small palm clattered in the heat but Jesús took me by the sleeve and drew me across the room. On a shelf over the stove stood a picture of Socorro and Jesús taken in a studio. "Something happened," he said. "It was at the washing place. Even while the children played in the suds. Even though it was always a good place without cars or animals or broken glass. Then this. Two men came and threatened her."

"Where is she? Is she safe?"

"Yes. She ran."

"Where's the baby, where's Elena?"

"Gone with her."

"Where did she go?" I asked. "Did she go home? Tell me the name. Tell me where it is."

"Zinacatán, in Chiapas," he told me, "where her mother is, and I am going too," he said, "but first we will sit together at the table. Like friends." He wiped his eyes. "When her mother said she had to be trained for marriage, she tried to demonstrate that being a woman does not mean being stupid. The way to avoid being stupid was to avoid getting married, so she thought becoming a nun was the way. And you shouldn't be too pretty, she thought. So she was wearing very ugly clothes when I met her, and trying all the time to pray. But I persisted. So look. She married me." He covered his wet eyes with his hands.

I climbed the stairs, holding the flowers which were not flowers at all, but parts of other things, the hand on hot skin, the forbidden fruit. The shirt on the stairs and the skin under the shirt and the flowers without scent and the dog that had come to live with us, that was as much one thing as another.

We drove away in the faded car with a dog and a child. The car had been repaired with a song and a prayer. "Take it slow," they had said, drawing pictures for us with their hands of the possible consequences if we drove too fast. But the dog was entirely pleased. And Alexander? Who could say? Alexander was the envy of everyone at La Casa. He was going north, although it was hard to believe. "Take your extra shirt, *niño!*" Señora Hidalgo cried, handing him a paper bag as Turner bundled him into the front seat with me. Two shirts, a pair of cotton pants, and bare feet, not unusual in Mexico. It wasn't our place to give him false expectations.

We were supposed to be met at Laredo, in a border hotel, at a certain time, so we watched the sun and the watch Turner wore, a watch he said he'd been given by his father when he turned thirteen. We watched the journey of the fire planet across the sky and the journey of two hands on the wrist. Along with that, we watched the surprising uninterest of the boy who sat on my lap.

Alexander stared as the small town faded away. He held himself upright at the open window and played with the lock button on the windowsill, up down, up down. Maybe he had nothing to compare this moment to, unless it was the other journey, the first one, when he was taken away from his people, whoever they were.

I thought of Socorro far away in the mountains of Chiapas. She'd left the Judas figure behind, and as we left Jesús had hung it outside over our iron gate and it swung there listlessly, as if warning all other Judases away.

Beyond Tequisquiapan there wasn't much for Alexander to focus on. We passed a man walking slowly up the highway, carrying a cross, a penitent, but Alexander hardly noticed. He noticed animals, and once he got excited about a cloud of smoke — a peasant, dressed in white, was burning his field. The black ground was smoldering and we were caught in a thicket of fumes that raced across our path. When Alexander saw the smoke he jerked upright and began to pant. His eyes widened and he pointed, not with his finger but with his chin. "Erererer," he said, moving up and down on my knee.

"Something's wrong with him."

"I think he has to pee."

"Not here," Turner said. "This smoke's all over us. What a stupid fucking thing to do." Turner was edgy. Two days, absolutely no more, to the border, he kept saying. Otherwise we might miss our connection.

"What are we going to do after that?"

"I don't know. Go back to school."

"They won't let you register."

"They might. If not I'll just live under my new false name." He laughed. "In highschool I made myself a false ID card so I could buy booze. I made myself from Manitoba somewhere, eighteen, the whole bit, but I misspelled Registration. And I'd even printed it in red." He changed the subject. "I wonder what Alexander's new life will be like. Imagine him living in Texas after that terrible place."

"It's what they're used to. They have mats to sleep on. They get fed. At least they're safe."

"How old is he, do they think?"

"Maybe six. He can touch his ear already."

"What's that mean?"

"When they can put one arm over their head and touch the opposite ear, that means they're six, that's all. They have to be six to be able to do that physically."

We moved across the terrain and through the thin air that carried more scent than nourishment. On every corner in every village a papier-mâché Judas hung over a doorway, leering down as we passed. Alexander was heavy on my lap, but at least there was the air. We all began to sniff at it, and the dog got up on his hind legs in the back and put his forepaws on the window ledge like Alexander. His tongue lolled nervously out of his long mouth. His eyes caught the play of light on a passing bus, and the shapes of the passengers who traveled in dreamlike connection with us. His ears bent forward to distinguish the sounds of the motor and tires. The dog tasted the diesel air and pulled it into his lungs with his long nose. He rode behind Turner and leaned out the window on the left, while Alexander sat on my lap and leaned out the window on the right. "It's the end of Alexander's past," I said.

"I doubt it," Turner said. "He'll always carry that sack of garbage around with him someplace in his brain, just like the rest of us. We're all the same. Give us the same food, the same bed, the same parents, and we'd be him." He stared out at the land, parched and overworked and ruined. No trees. No topsoil. Where was the dream Cortez had found?

I said, "My grandmother says all our bones will come together at the end."

"I thought it was dust to dust."

"According to her, on Judgment Day we'll climb out of our graves in our shoes and socks." Alexander felt large and warm against my emptiness. "Turner? What if at the border the river parts for everyone but us?"

In the middle of the afternoon Turner said, "We should eat," but it was Holy Thursday and there was nothing open. In one place we saw a line of small girls dressed in white, but the stores and businesses were closed. Like the saints — all week they'd been covered. There were no bells. The towns and villages were as silent as Alexander, who was sprawled across my lap, asleep with his head in the crook of my arm.

Finally we found an open restaurant. Outside it, there was a procession. People holding banners up, and two or three young boys on horseback, wearing short, white suits and red hoods with holes for their eyes, blowing whistles derisively. We cut through the line, leaving the dog in the car and pulling the child along. "We should sell the car and buy an ass," Turner said, "for this flight." In the empty restaurant, he picked up a knife and tapped it against his plate. A waitress appeared and in a few minutes we were eating small strips of beef covered in tomatoes and onions, pulling *tortillas* from a cloth-lined basket. After lunch Turner lifted Alexander to his shoulders and we went outside as a mob of Roman soldiers rounded the corner and a man with a spear in his hand rode past. *"Mira, Alexander! Qué es?"*

On the square in front of the lopsided church, a little fair had been set up. Platforms were being constructed for the Passion play and women were selling food. Men were having their hair cut under trees by sidewalk barbers.

"What are they up to?"

"Socorro told me this is the day they look for Jesus. Maybe they're Pharisees."

There were three tables with religious articles and pieces of clothing and there was Alexander, who shifted and jerked on Turner's shoulders. "It's a raffle. You get a ticket with a number. *Cuanto?*"

A thousand pesos.

"What will it be? The candle? The box of nails?" Turner dug a bill out of his pocket and knelt down so that Alexander could dismount. But Alexander pointed at a pair of boy's shoes, black, with ties. He stared at them as if they were an apparition sprung from the deepest recesses of his heart.

"They're not his size," Turner said.

"Never mind. Let him try."

Alexander took the soft bill from him, the greatest amount he'd ever held, and walked to the woman with the basket full of tickets, handing the money over, looking up briefly, not at me but at the clear, hot sky, while the woman swirled a fist around inside the basket. She wore long braids, a white blouse, an apron over her dark skirt. Alexander, she announced, had won a box of cereal on the first table. Women in braids and sombreros, holding babies like lumps of clay — babies who asked for nothing, who didn't cry — stood around us as Alexander walked up to the table uncertainly to claim his prize.

At the corner of the church a photographer was setting

up his camera. He had a stuffed donkey with a picture of the Virgin de Guadalupe hanging behind it. Alexander and Turner sat down on a tiled bench and watched the children being brought over by their parents. The donkey was a wooden form covered in skins. The Virgin was an image but she is always an image. The photographer threw a cloth over his head, then the shutter snapped. In a day or two there would be a picture of the little girl in her scarf pinned up on the board and her parents would come to retrieve it.

"We should get one of Alexander," Turner said.

"But he won't be back. He'll never get to see it."

"He doesn't know what the man's doing. All he knows is what he sees. He wants to be like the other kids."

Alexander watched the other children sitting on the donkey in front of the man with the box. He watched them being lifted up, posed, then set down again. When Turner carried him over to the back of the donkey and put him down, fixing his bare legs on each side of the furry back, he sat there majestically, the way the other children had. We paid the photographer and he took a picture of Alexander holding his box of cereal.

I wanted to go on this way a little longer, a man a woman a child.

In the evening we stopped again, having looked out at a thousand shrines along the highway bearing crosses and flowers, each one a memory of death. One day all the graves will open and Alexander will find his real mother, and also a woman who held him for hours in a small car with a man and a dog, I thought. He was asleep on my shoulder by then, his breath as rough as sand against my throat. I thought about my own child. What would it have looked like? Turner had green eyes. Mine were brown. The place where the metal had opened me still burned. If I hadn't believed in the baby before, I had to believe in it now.

In the little *zócalo*, the twelve apostles were gathered under a tree at a rough table outside the church. They looked like old men in white cotton suits, but they were being served by a young man in cloth trousers and leather shoes. We watched as a priest came out of the church and washed the feet of each apostle with a cloth, then kissed them.

In the street a boy rolled a tire along beside us, chasing our car. We found a pension with rooms around a courtyard and a parrot in a cage. There were the marks of hoofs on the beaten path, and an agave plant whose heart had been taken out so that it could be served to us for breakfast. Turner carried the silent child inside to a whitewashed room. All day he had been with us, and never a word.

"He's asleep. Put him down on the bed."

"Has he ever slept on one?"

"No." I stretched out beside the child.

"If you were going on a long trip and could only take three things, what would you take?" Turner said, sitting down and stroking my arm.

"You go first."

"Me, I'd take a dictionary, a Baby Ruth, and a...."

"Rose! I'd take you. And Alexander. And a dog."

Turner lay beside me on his back, his arms up, his eyes with their violet lids closed against the moonlight, and we smelled the thick Mexican walls of the room, a damp and dry smell, a smell of clay. He put his mouth against my belly and moved his face down, down toward my other mouth, but I pushed him away. In the darkness I heard drums but there were other things to keep me awake. The rough breathing of the child, who was sleeping at last in an actual bed. The long body of the man who lay beside me on this narrow mattress meant for one. The thought of Kate waiting farther away, sleeping alone. A mosquito visited the boy and I covered him. Every few minutes the whine of the insect came back when he had thrown off the sheet again. I thought of the thing that had been inside me and was gone.

The next morning we followed the road through the desert of San Luis Potosí to the border. According to our papers, we were parents. The false papers carried false names. Sticks and stones. But the river lay ahead, waiting to be crossed, and the papers were our only means of entry. Then the hotel in Laredo where we'd give Alexander up to his Texas family. I was tired of his chin digging into my shoulder and I was tired of the way he held on to me. I was tired of the sand blowing through the car window, piling up on my skin. I was tired of my skin, too. It would be a relief to be able to take off my body like a blouse. Turner was right — there was no place for a child in our lives. The car was too crowded, what with the dog and the bottles and the spare tire and the bag. But still, I was growing attached to this silent companion.

For a long time we drove on, leaving no mark or sign of our passing.

Then, out of nowhere, a woman appeared on the highway, covered in cloth, and Turner swerved wildly and cursed. He pulled over and flung his door open but when he looked back there was no sign of her. "Did you feel anything?"

"No."

"But you saw her? That old woman back there? Did we brush her or not?"

I craned around and peered through the rear window. "I don't know."

Turner slammed his door and dropped his head to the steering wheel. He'd hardly spoken for hours. I thought it must be the border ahead, although perhaps it was me. Perhaps he was wishing I hadn't come, after all. "We should go back and take a look," he said. But neither of us moved. "We should have been in Laredo hours ago. The border's only safe at certain hours."

"You never told me that."

Turner opened the door again and got out of the car. He was limping, digging into his pockets and flinging something into the ditch. But it was only a handful of Mexican coins. I could hear them ringing against a piece of metal sunk in the ground. "What do you mean?" I shouted. "Our papers should do the trick, shouldn't they?" The dog started barking. Alexander was whimpering. Maybe he has to pee again, I thought, grabbing him and pulling him out of the car. "Turner? Is this more complicated than you said?" He was standing in the middle of the highway with his back to me. "What else did you forget to tell me?"

"Nothing. But say we get charged. With kidnapping, say, or false entry or anything."

Turner in his faded jeans, his white shirt, his cowboy boots, his hands. Sweating. A light haze over the river ahead where the slaughterhouses lay. The great bridge crossing that stench, leaving the flat grasses of Mexico and entering the concrete folds of Texas, and Turner turning around and walking back to the car again. Ahead of us was the buckled, brown body of water, plunging on from its beginning to its end, rushing in its untired exhaustion east, south, into the gulf, cutting the continent.

Alexander was still whimpering as he walked back to the car, even though he'd taken his small penis out of his pants and watered one side of the highway. Out here, his trickle of urine would evaporate in seconds. It would never reach the river rushing, cutting through the afternoon, dividing us from the next thing, the clutch and brake released, the car in reverse and Turner pulling back onto the highway.

Twenty minutes later we took our place in a line of cars and approached the checkpoint, Alexander turning his face into my blouse, closing his eyes. A new mother and father, I whispered in Spanish. But he shook his head and went into the cave under my arm. "Put a hat on him, to hide the hair at least," Turner said grimly. Stiff, black. Hair from another tribe. "Put the clean shirt on him too." As if we were responsible for the dark hair and dark skin. As if the shirt would change anything.

I reached for the paper sack. But the inspector leaned into the car at that moment, passing a flashlight over us and over our false tourist cards, and I felt warm water on my legs and an instant shame, as if I'd wet myself. "Shit! Alexander!"

"Americans?"

Yes. With a paper sack and a pack and a suitcase and a dog. And a child. We were part of Turner Hays now, registered, stamped, sealed, and almost delivered, except that what was waiting ahead was a low, flat building, ugly, like a warehouse baking in the sun.

We were being escorted. I kept looking back. Were they searching the car? I was worried about the dog. I wondered if the man who was behind us knew about Mr. Hogan, or if Mr. Hogan had paid off the men in the customs building.

I wondered how many people worked for Mr. Hogan. Maybe everyone did. Turner carried Alexander. Just behind them, the customs officer walked briskly. Which side had Gus Hogan worked on with his money? This man didn't look like the type to be worked on by anyone. "I told you I'm not lucky," Turner said over his shoulder.

"You told that to Kate. You never gave me any warning."

"My wife's not feeling too well," Turner told the officer when we got inside.

The man looked at me. He reddened slightly. "The fact is," he muttered, "we're just wondering about the little boy." The man was young, pink, his nose a short stub. He was trained against Mexicans, hippies. The pink face peered at Alexander, who was staring at the man's black, shiny shoes. "Why?" said Turner softly. "Because he's adopted?"

The man put a finger out to Alexander, as if he expected the boy to grab it. "You want to come in and lay down? You got some papers for that dog back there?" he said to me, taking the tourist card out of my hand.

I shook my head. Turner put Alexander down. "I'm soaked," he said. The cards were carried over to a counter, then back of it to a desk. There were some dusty files stacked on it but the man didn't open them. He bent over our cards and examined them. He looked at us. "You're young to be bringing up a kid, aren't you." He picked up the phone, then put it down. "Something's not right here," he said, straightening. "I can't let you take the boy in. We've been having some problems with kids. Fake adoptions. A prostitution ring. You folks may be fine. I can't say about that. But if so you got nothing to worry about. You can come back on Tuesday, after the holiday. The supervisor can maybe do something for you but I'm not putting my neck on the line. Not with a kid like this."

I had broken into a sweat. Our surroundings were all cement, gray, barren, hard, a hideous doorway to America. We drove out of the parking lot. Heat rose in waves. The indifference of the landscape could be felt like the weather. Across the river Laredo glimmered like the Promised Land, tall as a ship with windows, where the fathers of the country sat over ledgers and deeds while farmers, ranchers, truckers brought their goods in to be purchased, steaming, hot, alive.

The first thing Turner did was pull up in front of a bar. It was Good Friday. The town was muffled. Most of the businesses were closed, but Turner found a place that was open. And it had a phone. It was hot but there was an electric fan. Turner rattled some coins in his pocket, ordered two beers and a Coke, and, when they were in front of us, got up to use the phone. "I'll call the hotel in Laredo," he told me. When he came back he said, "Nobody's waiting for Alexander. They chickened out because we're late. But they'll be back. They have to be. Sooner of later. Otherwise we're stuck with this kid...." Turner lit a cigarette and stubbed it out. "Something else," he said, his eyes turned away from mine.

"What? Tell me."

"Kate knows where I am. She found out my whereabouts."

"How?"

"She found out... Lily, she's over there. What am I supposed to do now?"

"Did you talk to her?"

"I got the guy on the phone to recommend a place for us

tonight. He's giving her the phone number. So she can get in touch with us. Me," he corrected himself.

"You? She doesn't know I'm with you?"

"She doesn't know anything."

We finished our beers and left. The next thing Turner did was go to a store that had shoes lined up according to size. "For the Texas sidewalks," he told Alexander, leaving us outside in the oven-like car.

I watched him through the store window, bending down, selecting, measuring a shoe against his own palm. I thought about how Turner had disappeared a year before, taking off for the spring break and not coming back. I thought about the party in the mountains and what I'd done and what he would have to tell Kate. I thought about seeing her. I looked out at the listless town. A small group of penitents went by at the end of the street. I thought about Socorro but there was no name for what I felt. I'd caused her troubles and my own and Turner's and Kate's.

When Turner emerged from the store with a pair of red high-top sneakers in a white box, Alexander's dark, sleepy eyes opened wide. He dropped the box of cereal and let me slip the high-tops on his feet, banging them together before they were even tied. For a minute we forgot our troubles. We watched Alexander and even smiled. Then Turner started-ed the car again and we drove past a group of worshippers on their way to church.

Finally we went to the shabby hotel with a porch and a broken door. There was the smell of old food. There was a short hall, a room with some chairs and a desk, some cabinets full of salvaged things, a picture of the Virgin standing on a crescent moon. Turner spoke to the old woman who ran the place. Alexander stood in his new shoes with his

paper sack. I thought we would walk up the stairs to a dark-
ened room with this dark-haired boy who didn't belong to
us. The hotel was old but our rooms would be clean. It
would have a bedspread and matching curtains. It would
have a double bed because Turner would want to cover me
with clean, white sheets and with his own flesh, which was
brown from the desert of San Luis Potosí. In that way, we
would wait. But the old woman said, "*Su esposa*," and
pointed upstairs. Turner looked at me blankly. Had he told
the old woman we were married? Had he employed the false
name?

The old woman handed Turner a room key. I kept my
head down as we moved across the blotched linoleum and
went up the narrow stairs.

What light there was stayed behind us as we opened the
door to the room, and I moved carefully, tripping over
something, a metal wastebasket and hitting the side of a
small bed with my knees. I reached down to feel the bed
and touched a body.

"Lily!" Kate was lying there on the bed in the dark. She
sat up and pushed the button on the bedside lamp. She
looked at both of us and there was pleasure and pain in the
look, then she put her arms around me. "Lily, honey! Why
didn't he tell me he'd found you?" She'd cut her hair and she
was wearing nylons although Turner didn't like short hair
and he didn't like nylons either. She'd been on a train and
then on a bus. "It was terrible," she told us. "I'm a wreck. I
can never sleep sitting up." My teeth were chattering. I
clenched my jaw. Turner walked over to the corner of the
room, while I stood by the bed, holding Alexander's hand.
Kate said, "Who's that?"

"He's from the place where I worked. He's going to Texas

to get adopted." I dropped the small hand. "Alexander," I said. Kate put hers out to him and he crossed the space between them and pointed down. "*Zapatos!*" he said firmly, as if he'd been talking all his life.

"Alexander Zapatos?"

"No, he means shoes!" I looked at Turner. "Did you hear that?"

Alexander's first word seemed more unbelievable even than the sudden appearance of Kate, but he straightened his back and shook Kate's hand, standing formally in front of her, almost knee to knee, then breaking into a sudden, wonderful laugh.

"What's going on?" Turner said uneasily, staring at him.

Alexander put his hand over his mouth, as if his happiness had to be contained. Then I realized his mistake. "Alexander thinks Kate's about to be a mother," I said. Turner's head jerked up. I doubt if Kate even saw it, but no wonder our little charge was happy! Even nervous and exhausted, Kate was glowing, her hair shiny and clean, her face — her expression — completely unarmed. "It's a natural mistake. It's kind of confusing, all this driving around looking for a family."

"What an idea," Kate said seductively, reaching down to lift Alexander up on her knees. "Oh," she said faintly, then, "he kind of smells."

Turner kicked his boots off. "We all do," he said blandly.

"We should give him a nice bubble bath. Would he like that?" Kate said. "And Turner, I told my folks about this," Kate continued, standing up and going over to him. "So if it makes you feel any better, at least we don't have to sneak around. I told them I was coming down here but I had an important reason."

He put his arms around her and kissed her briefly. "What reason?" he said, turning away and wandering over to the bed she had left. "And how did you find me? I can't believe you came all the way down here. What about classes?"

Kate sat down on the only chair, while Alexander reached up and put both hands into her hair and settled against her. She smiled at him and stretched her legs out so that through the skirt they made an angle with her body. In the dark room she looked like a letter, a piece of the alphabet, an inverted Y. "Isabel got hold of somebody named Hogan."

Turner looked over at her apprehensively. "Why get Isabel to call Hogan. You knew I was coming back. What was so unbelievably important suddenly? "

I thought Isabel might have told Turner where I was for one reason only — to give us, or the child we might have had, a chance. But why would she have told Kate where we were? At least I knew she hadn't told her why I'd come. That much was obvious.

"Because I had to give you something. But don't get all negative when you see it. I have a plan. I know we can work everything out."

Turner said nothing.

"It's a letter," Kate said, without making any effort to produce it. "And it came registered. It's your notice to report. That's what I told Isabel. That's why we called Mexico. Because you've already missed your physical." She turned to face me. "Lil, Turner and I need to talk a little bit," she said quietly. "Oh Lil, I'm so glad you're here. I was scared stiff about you. But…I…I've come so far to talk to him. And I need…" She turned to face the bed again, moving just the top part of the Y. Then she looked at me. "…I need to be alone with him."

I walked over to the window. There were two layers of drapes across it, some gauzy fabric underneath the heavy stuff. I pulled all of them back and stared out so she wouldn't see my face.

"I'll bet he's never had ice-cream," Kate said. "This little boy. Has he? Why don't I buy him one?" She reached for her purse, which was on the floor.

"You don't have that kind of money," Turner blurted out. I considered that. He didn't seem very glad to see her.

"What?"

"Mexican."

"I'm sure they'll take this." Kate opened the purse and dug around in it. Without looking up she fished out a dime and thrust it at Alexander, who plucked it up between his finger and thumb, the thinnest of currencies. I remembered how we had set traps for other children, for Clare and a couple of boys in the neighborhood. We told Clare there was a kitten crying in the tunnel that ran under the street; then we left her in the dark. We told the boys there were pictures in the tunnel, pictures we weren't allowed to see. I knew what Kate was doing. But in a moment I was outside with Alexander on the hot sidewalk, looking up at the rented room. The door opened and the old woman came out on her way to the church, her head covered with a dark veil. The car still sat at the curb and the dog was asleep in it. The windows were smudged, but I could see him curled up in there and overhead, in the hotel room, Kate was trying to talk to the man she loved. "Something happened," he was probably saying. "I need to explain things to you."

I knew Kate. She wouldn't make any demands. She'd try to comfort him. She would realize he was afraid. "Just come here…first…no, I'm coming over there," she'd say, dropping onto the bedspread next to him. In a minute, Turner would tell her about the letter he'd meant to send — the one I'd found — but while he talked she'd be rubbing her mouth across his and testing his edges, which had been so familiar only a few days before. He'd feel the world wavering. "I had to talk to you in person," she'd say, because why else had she come? She'd say, "I know things are going to be okay."

But what would Turner say? Would he mention the party? He'd fumble over that. He'd put his feet in their torn socks on the ground next to the bed. I could already see him standing up. He wasn't going to stay up there alone with her. He would find an excuse to get back to me. He'd tell her he had to check the dog. He'd think of something. I waited. I'd forgotten the ice-cream and I'd forgotten Alexander, who was staring up as hungrily as I was.

There was a place just inside the door of the hotel, a little hallway where we stood when we went back in. In a few minutes Turner came slouching down the stairs with Kate trailing behind. "It doesn't have to be so terrible," I heard her say. "Come on, we can beat this, I know we can. We have some alternatives."

"What alternatives do you conceive of?" Turner said sharply.

"I spied a young cowboy all dressed in white linen," Kate said, coming up behind him and putting her arms around his back. She pulled him against her. "Marriage works in most states," she said.

I couldn't see Turner's face but I heard him say, "Why didn't my mother send it sooner?"

"Your mother? She did. The letter came to her house and she sent it on to school, but I guess it just lay there in the mailroom. You didn't go in to pick your mail up. And then you were gone. Then Pearson — he came back and saw it and picked it up and gave it to me because he thought I might know where you were."

Turner pulled one arm free of her and looked at the skin on the inside of it absently. "I'm staying down here," he said.

"So I came all this way for absolutely nothing?" Kate pushed herself around to face him and put her hand palm to palm against his, as if she wanted to place herself in his care. "Don't leave me out of your life," she whispered. "Mexico won't work."

"If that's why you came, to get me to go square things with my draft board, you can forget it." Turner pulled away and started across the lobby crookedly.

"I came because I need you."

"I'm not getting drafted, Kate. I'd rather go to jail."

"You don't know what you're even talking about. Mexico doesn't solve anything. They can deport you."

"I don't know anything any more." Turner had turned away, but Kate followed him and put her arm through his and took him to the corner, where they sat down. There was an ashtray on a stand there.

Turner pawed at it and brought out a curled, unbroken, half-smoked cigarette. "Light?" he said.

A young boy, who must have been standing inconspicuously behind the desk, came forward, holding out a thin book of matches that appeared to have been in his back pocket, just above the place where he sat, for days. The boy didn't light the cigarette but he waited to have the matchbook back and then swiftly put it away again. Then he stood there, close to Turner and Kate, waiting for them to get on with things. He probably thought it wouldn't hurt to be nice to a girl like that. After all, why get her here to a hotel if you didn't expect the demands a girl like that makes? He'd already seen plenty of girls, and this one was a serious type. She took a risk coming, by the looks of this guy with the hair and two-day beard. And the other one, the one with the kid. She was with them but kind of lost, the way she drifted around. The boy moved a few steps closer to Kate and Turner, as if they were magnets and he was drawn to them. "What if I remind you that I belong with you?" Kate said very quietly. Turner lit another butt from the ashtray and stubbed the first one out. "Couldn't we be alone for a few minutes?" she said. "Please. I need to hold you."

"Kate, I have a kid to worry about," Turner said. He took a long drag and flicked the burning filter he was holding into the ashtray. "Things are going crazy in my life right now."

I stood in the little hallway listening to everything, because I was part of them. They were my life. Kate said, "Turner, I'm not letting you out of my sight for a single second ever again. I mean that. If you're doing something, I'm doing it with you."

Turner said, "You might have to stay down here forever, then. I'm not going back up there to get drafted, Kate, and that's that."

"You can't hide down here. Legally. You have to go to Canada for that. Or Sweden. But there are other things we could do to at least show some intentions on your part. We could at least try and get you deferred. It would help if you were married. It would help to go back to school."

"First I have a few other things to think about. I have this kid, for one thing, who's supposed to be getting adopted right now and they won't let him into the States. And Lily. Don't forget her. And a dog."

Kate's voice was beginning to sound strained. "Turner. This is about your life! You missed your physical! What dog?"

"He's out in the car, probably about to suffocate. How much money have you got?"

"On me?"

"Where else is money?"

"After the bus ticket...forty-seven dollars, give or take."

"Let's go liberate the dog."

Kate smiled. She loved the craziness in Turner when it included her. It was like the growth of beard on his face. Behind it there was the good skin, the clean map. His lunacy was a disguise meant to promote privacy, but as long as she was inside it, she didn't mind.

"We're on our way out to release the dog," Turner explained, as they passed me in the hallway. "How was the ice-cream?" He scooped Alexander up and grabbed my hand.

When we got outside, he pointed to the car and it had its effect on Kate. Turner pulled the door open and the dog jumped out and ran up and down the sidewalk. Kate said, "Here, honey...." She had a voice to call things. "Here, boy. We should get him some water," she pointed out.

"Turner?... Where's the bowl?" I said. "You wedged it in here someplace this morning, didn't you? Or was it last night?" I was going to make my point now. I was going to make my claim. Turner handed it to me and we started up the sidewalk, although Alexander began to drag his feet and pull at Kate's hand. Maybe this wasn't the life he wanted, after all. Maybe Kate wasn't the mother he wanted, either. We pulled him after us and crossed at the light. Kate said, "You know, I think your mother actually wanted you to get drafted." She turned to me. "I don't know what to do, Lil, I mean, he got called for his physical and didn't show. That's why I came down here. To tell him. If he doesn't do something, either get back in school, which it's probably too late to do, or something else, he's had it. They're supposed to notify their draft board if they're going out of the country or anything. And then he was on probation and he didn't come back to school. They're hunting them down, the guys who are using college as an excuse. One minor mistake and they're after you." Alexander suddenly stopped in his tracks and Kate focused on him. "Come on, honey," she said, as she'd said to the dog. Turner didn't stop for us. I wanted to run up the sidewalk with him, but Kate stood there holding Alexander's hand. She said, "I don't really think me getting married to him is the answer right now, but I'll do it if it gives him back his safety. It's not how I wanted it, Kate…how we used to imagine it…." She stood looking down at her sandals. "It's not that silk wedding dress in Jensons or anything, but if I don't at least provide some ideas, he's going to do something stupid and I'll never see him again."

Up ahead, swiping his arm at the sky, Turner signaled — come. And I ran. He was nervous. He didn't look at me. "What's she doing, for Christ's sake?" he asked.

"She's not doing anything. She's telling me how she's going to save you."

There was a drinking fountain at the corner. We filled the water bowl and put the dog back in the car, then wandered back to the hotel, where the light was thick with dust and with other things, old smoke, too much love lost in the corridors and seeping out. We narrowed our eyes, Kate still clean, still bright in her summer dress with her drawstring red leather bag. The dress was yellow and it had small tucks across the front. A dress of anytime, out of time, and Kate's hair, too, was catching the light as she bent forward examining something about her hem. Turner was crouched beside her, caught in the light she held. They spoke. Yes, no, yes, no, leaning together. "Why don't you check Lily in?" Kate said at one point. The light, how long would it last? What would we do when it left us? Turner went across the lobby to the desk, which had fallen into shadow. The old woman had returned. "Room?"

Turner nodded.

"Bueno," the woman said. There was a stool and her large behind balanced on it, the dismal Virgin on the wall. The smell of old, smoked cigarettes. "You want two rooms or three?" she said, naming her price.

"You take dogs?"

"*Cómo? Los perros? No!*"

"Two rooms then," Turner said, and we went up the stairs, defeated by the doors ahead. We were going to go on as before, of course, but which before? When?

"This is silly," said Kate, stopping at a door, because Turner had moved away, taking another one. She must have realized that he meant for her to sleep with me. She stood with her hand out, a small key held in it, and a tremor of disappointment went through her, I saw it. Dark green linoleum. Heavy ceiling overhead and the narrow passage. The windowless, corrupt air which had been through a thousand nights. The dress all folds now and Kate's arm, wrist, hand. The realization as she stood there, turning the key, unlocking her room, that Turner was thinking of me. But she pulled me in. "Let's order us some Thunderbird. They must have it around here someplace, don't you think? Call up room service and let's run this little boy a bath."

Turner would go outside again and bring in our dog wrapped in the green serape. But I sat on the floor with Alexander undressing him. After all these days together, I put my hands on his small body the color of wood and it smelled bitter. Even the breath from his mouth was harsh. I unbuttoned his shirt and let it drop to the floor. It was filthy. I pulled off the red sneakers. But he tried to put them back on again.

"Look," Kate said simply. "We'll all do it." She pulled off her dress and underwear and stood in front of him. She said, "Come on," and went in to run a bath. I pulled Alexander, crying now, to the tub, where the heat of the water alarmed him. He drew back when I put his hand in but when Kate climbed in he touched it furtively. She put soap in her hair and did the same thing to him, smiling at his fear and at the roughness of his skin.

"There now," she said, "why don't you two get in?"

I was afraid to take my clothes off, as if something might be visible, but I eased Alexander into the bath and took off my dress and underpants and climbed into the water with them. I was sore. I looked down at my empty body. My knees jolted up out of the water, but Kate leaned against the tiles, her head back against the damp wall. "Would you believe I sat up all night with a sailor in the dome car? I can hardly see straight, I'm so tired, but something came over me and I just couldn't bear to be alone. Do you ever get that feeling? I needed somebody to be with me."

"I know what you mean."

Alexander sat in the water, watching us. "You're not used to it like I am, though. I'm spoiled," Kate went on. "Since Turner came back to school, I've been with him all the time." She looked at me. No tremor this time. Just darker eyes. "Oh, there's our Thunderbird at the door. And the sandwiches. *Tortas*. Should I go? Could the little boy get it? No, I'll have to sign. That should give the old lady or her grandson a thrill." Kate got out and wrapped herself in a small towel. When she came back in with the bottle, she unscrewed the cap of the Thunderbird. "Move over. Maybe we can cook whatever ails us," she said. "It's been awhile, huh? Cheers. We should tell Turner to come in, too." She laughed uneasily.

Alexander pulled himself out and stumbled into the bedroom, but we sat in the hot water and drank. Our clothes were everywhere. Half an hour together, and the room was excessive. Wine spilled into us like blood, each of us holding back the growing darkness so that the grizzled wall with its lost tiles, the vaporous room, the marked floor, grim basin and toilet, lies and love were silvered by the dusk.

At last, just to lie down, to find the bed and the boy lying there on the spread, which had been repaired, and under which the bottom sheet was worse, as coarse as pavement. "Tell me," said Kate, "what Turner was like down there."

"*Down there?*" This old term for our cavities, our sex. We were lying side by side, as bare as trees in spring.

She giggled. "Down here, I mean! Mexico." Her body was thin, the color of wheat. When she moved, lifted an arm or leg, it was as if wind were striking. I had run away because I loved her. I should have told her that. But so much stood between us now. The body of a man. Desire. Even the gloved hands holding metal. Even this child. No longer girls now, but women, we lay together, matching our hipbones, our steamy flesh. Kate rolled over to face me. She reached over my shoulder and poured more wine into her glass. "I'm trying to understand, Lil. You have to tell me. Why did you run away?"

I remembered standing outside the party with her. "Something happened," I said. I loved her skin. But it wasn't mine. It wasn't even related to me. I lay there looking at her face, the short, dark hair, the shoulders that showed her bones. "Come on, you're not drinking," she said, putting her mouth over mine and opening it, pouring her own wine into me. For a moment I felt inhabited again. "You don't have to be afraid. I'm not as perfect as you think," she said. "The only difference is, I know what I want." She put her hands on my back and ran them down my body, as if I were her woman brother, her alien twin. She said, "Your grandmother's getting old, you should go back home. You have to live with your own kind." The smell of heated flowers wafted in over us. Tuberose. I was beginning to feel savage. "I hope you don't love him," Kate said.

Later Turner came in quietly and stood looking down at our bodies, bare and grown together. Mine had been cleaned of everything. I was no longer threatening. But Kate's was still full of her faith in him.

When we lifted our heads, Alexander was eating, hunched over a tray. The curtains were open, blowing, and the two windows were facing the bed. Between them there was a dresser, a mirror, a tray of sandwiches. No light but the sky reflecting light from the streets below.

In the morning, Turner got up, pulled on his jeans and tapped on our door. "Let's go eat."
Kate kept her eyes shut. "Let him in," she said, but she got up and went to the bathroom. "Did you tell her anything?" Turner whispered, when I opened the door.
"I can't," I said.

Outside, we found the car again, and Turner remembered to cross the *guardacoche*'s palm as Kate opened the door. "Where are we supposed to sit?" she asked, but she got in and crouched in the back and Turner pulled away from the curb, with the radio coming on and the dog standing up on the floor of the car. Saturday morning. This is when the Mexicans celebrate Easter. The little resurrection. "I'm starving," said Kate, sitting back on the tire and gazing out. She was American in the way some Americans are. She didn't see the flesh of the earth stripped, the bones left bare. She saw what she wanted to see.

We found a restaurant. "Sit by the door where we can keep an eye on things," Turner said.

"Like what?" Kate sat down beside him and unfolded her napkin. She looked around. "Are you getting paranoid? Your only problem in the world is your draft board and nobody's going to arrest you over eggs and toast." A waitress was approaching, but Kate went right on. She said, "It's too bad I'm not pregnant, Turner; that would get you off. From what I hear it works like a charm." For a minute the room went out of focus. I lost my breath. "Good morning please," said the waitress, who was carrying paper menus but forgot to offer them. Her English reminded me of my classroom and I looked over at Alexander, but he gave no sign of having heard. Turner sighed. He ordered a beer and pressed his foot against mine. Kate ordered coffee. *"Y cuatro huevos rancheros,"* I said, hoping she'd notice my accent. It crossed my mind that Turner might be pressing her foot too, but apparently he was meditating. "Then Alexander doesn't count as my problem?" he said, working on his beer, which had come as if by instinct.

"He's not yours. If they won't let him in the States, call that place where Lily worked and tell them to pick him up. We have to get back. I've got school." Turner didn't appear to be listening. He was shifting on his chair, crossing and uncrossing his legs, scratching his neck. "The thing I don't get is why the people who want this little boy don't just come over here," Kate went on.

Turner looked at her. He said. "We don't have their names," as if he were ashamed of the fact. "We just knew where we were supposed to meet. And where I was supposed to get paid."

"For what?"

"For doing this. Getting him over there."

"What are you two doing? Bringing in illegal aliens?"

"Maybe. But they're just kids. The papers are fixed. It's no big deal."

"What papers?" Kate was preparing a smile. She wanted to understand.

"To get us back in. With Alexander." Even while he was talking, Turner's attention seemed to be someplace else. "They say Lily's my wife. And he's our kid. Only it's not my real name. And they didn't work. Which is why we're stuck in this sleazy piece of shit restaurant trying to get something to eat. Because in order to facilitate the ordinary experience of crossing a river, one of God's little boundaries, we had to go to that extreme, and now they'll be watching for us at the border."

Kate said, "You're entering your own country with forged documents, when you're already in enough trouble to go to jail?"

Turner's second beer arrived, then our food. "But that makes sense," Kate went on, as the plates were being set down, "assuming there's a million dollars waiting for you or you go straight to heaven when you cross the river."

"Or Alexander does."

Alexander was staring at his eggs. Kate moved his plate. Sitting him up straight, like a big doll, she gave him a fork. He was not going to eat with his hands, not in front of her. "I find this all very strange," she said to no one in particular, concentrating on tucking Alexander's napkin into his shirt. "I'm beginning to feel like I shouldn't be here. Why is that?"

Turner glared at me. Maybe I was supposed to say something or maybe I was the one who was out of place.

Whatever my obligations were, the longer I sat there, the emptier I felt.

"Then there's the dog to consider," Turner remarked. "We can't just leave him down here." He shoved his chair back, extending his legs under the table knocking Kate's coffee cup over, and a pitcher of syrup. The liquids ran across her plate and splashed onto Alexander. Sticky. Hot. He wailed.

"It's on his legs," Kate cried, standing up and grabbing him.

"Ice," Turner said.

I handed him a glass of water but Alexander went on crying as Kate and Turner dabbed at him. He got off his chair and crouched by it.

We remembered to take some *tortillas* back to the car so the dog could eat, then Kate said, "Take Alexander back with you and wash him off. Get him in the tub if you can. We'll try the bridge again in an hour when the traffic starts going back and forth. Right now, Lily can walk with me. I want to look around. I've never been here before, you know. I want a chance to see what it feels like."

Turner did as he was told. "Something gorgeous is what I have in mind," Kate said, as he disappeared. "But you have to help. You have to talk him into it. Because we should do it fast and it might be easier to do it here than on the other side."

"Do what?"

"Get married. I don't think, down here, we even need a license." She took my arm. We walked up the filthy sidewalk. There were women all over Mexico walking arm in arm in the same way. Like sisters.

"Kate, listen. At school, when I left, it was because of Turner," I said.

"Oh, I know! You felt left out." She kept walking, kept hold of me. "After you were gone I felt terrible. I figured out how hard it must have been for you to be around us when we'd just found each other again. That's why I sent him down here, to make you feel more a part of us." Kate pulled something out of her purse — a thin envelope — and handed it to me. "I forgot I even had this because it came a while back. But Zozzie never writes so I thought it might be...."

"You sent Turner down?"

"Lily, I was scared for you!" Suddenly Kate stopped. "Hey, this could be it!" She pointed at a store window. "Look at the dress." It was white, cotton, with rows of tucks and lace.

"I don't feel left out," I said, standing very still, but Kate was pushing through the plastic beads that hung in the doorway and in a moment a woman in silver earrings was taking the dress off the mannequin. Then Kate was turning around in it. "I feel like a bride already," she said. The store was small and there were blouses and dresses and shawls hanging from hooks all the way to the ceiling. I could hardly breathe. *"Qué bonita!"* smiled the woman who worked there, sounding sincere. Kate got her billfold out. "Do you think he'll approve?"

In a minute, we were back in the sunlight with the dress folded up in a paper sack. "But what I want you to explain," she said, taking my arm again, "is how you got involved with all this."

I said. "Kate. What you said last night. About me loving Turner. Well, I do."

Turner was waiting for us in his hotel room when we got back, but someone was with him, someone familiar. "Mr. Santos," I said, "what're you doing here?" The dog ran over and jumped at me, as if we'd been gone for hours. Kate threw the sack with the dress in it on the bed and sat down, rigid. She was still waiting for my explanation, and she barely glanced at the intruder. Turner was silent. "Where's Alexander?" I said, looking around. The room, other than the bed with Kate's package on it, was as neat as a pin. Even Turner seemed not to be in it, and Santos was as stiff as the furniture. The curtains were closed again. The water glass on the dresser was under its cloth. There was not so much as a stray hair any place. Turner looked up. "Guess why he's here?" he said.

"To help us get across."

"Wrong. He wants us to give back the documents. So they won't be traced. He wants us to give back Alexander, too. So much for *la futura*!"

"Señorita," Santos broke in, "you have arrived at the wrong time yesterday. Now there is a situation with *Migración*. It is very difficult just now at the border where adoptions are concerned." The black cane was at his side, leaning on the wall by the bathroom door.

"Where's Alexander?" I asked, again.

"What about my money?" Turner said tightly, ignoring me.

"The clients are gone now. Also their money."

"*Their* money?" I said. "You mean...?" But Turner frowned and I caught his look. I had forgotten Kate; I was thinking about the child we might have had. Would they have sold her, too? Is that what they did? Turner focussed on the bed. "What's in the bag, Kate?"

"Nothing. Just a dress."

"We need your money to get out of here now." He stubbed his cigarette out. "Unless Santos here pays up." Still looking at Kate, he said "The kid's worth something to him, Lil, or he wouldn't be here. Right?"

"I am here to save all of us from trouble."

"Because they're looking for you up there? Because you want the documents and Alexander to disappear now? Was there ever a real adoption, Santos? Or is this the kiddie prostitution thing they told us about at the border. Is that where our silent Alexander was headed?"

"You should answer Lily's question," Santos said coldly. "The boy. He is in another room? Because if he is with you you are implicated in this."

"I thought you worked only for yourself, Santos, not Gus Hogan."

Santos made a small smile. "I get paid nothing from him."

"But you're paid for the kids, right? Cuban kids or whatever. Hogan launders it or you wash it out for him. You do each other's dirty underwear."

Santos grimaced. His jaw was so tight it flickered. "You

are holding my property. A little child. I feel sorry for him. He had some chance up there, if you think of that. People have money in Texas. But in Mexico? What life does he have? These are things you would put out of your mind. They're not pleasant to think. Each of us, *amigo*, must have a way to survive."

"Not like that."

I was watching Turner. But something caught my eye. A red shoe on the floor in the bathroom.

Santos coughed. "Otherwise he is nothing." He put his hand into his jacket and leaned forward as if he was experiencing a pain in his chest. But instead of the brown bottle of orange liquid, he pulled a small gun out of the inside pocket, moving his hand smoothly, as if he had practice doing this. "I must insist," he said softly.

I reached out. Pure instinct. Grabbing at the gun. But Santos pushed me back, and I fell. I remember crying out as I hit the floor and a weight fell on top of me. I heard his head smashing against the metal bed. The gun in my hand now, not his, and blood. It was warm. I had no air, no breath. I could feel his surprising bones pressing. And a sound I'd never heard, a strange sound and Turner above us holding the thin, hard cane but it was Kate who was making the noise. A high moan like grief. So I pushed Santos off me.

Turner got down on his knees and bent to peer into the space under the bed. "Come on!" I heard him saying. "It's okay." Then Alexander's small body slid out and I saw him framed by the doorway, which was open now and which held its light around his hair. It seemed to take timeless hours, all this. I seemed not to have any legs but I stood up and pulled my dress down and listened to my heart. Then we ran down the stairs.

We must have looked strange, all of us without bags, pouring out the door past the boy in the lobby, who looked astonished but not quite awake. The dog was running with us, too, as if he'd been trained for escapes. We got to the car and Kate shoved me inside, pulling the front seat forward so that Alexander fell in after me. She threw herself in and slammed the door while Turner got in with the dog and started the car.

In back there was still the pile of boxes, the tire, the old papers flying around. But now Alexander and I were crammed in as well, and Turner was driving fast. The wind was around us. Kate said, "Who was that?" as we hurtled around a corner, up a street. We were headed for the highway, the one that stretched north, south. Around us nothing but land that could never belong to anything. We drove across the desert and again Kate said, "Tell me what's going on? I can't stand this. Turner? Where are we going?"

"What fucking difference is it going to make?" Turner shouted. "I'm fucked now whatever happens, no matter what country I'm in. It's out of our hands."

Kate said venomously, "You were protecting Lily. What's so wrong with that?"

I was crouched on the tire, my lips pulled back. Ahead of us I saw Texas. Bleached. White. I knew Turner was afraid of it. And Kate was afraid of me.

"I told you," she reminded him softly, putting a hand on his shoulder. "We could go to Canada. They speak English up there, at least."

I felt a familiar pain. I knew I was sorry, but it wasn't for either of them. It was for myself, for my body that I'd betrayed. Turner and I had never belonged anyplace. Except

in the house of lightning, against the marble floors. Now
the bridge was ahead. There were trees lining the road on
either side. I remembered them from the day before, a life-
time away. I remembered the telephone poles I'd counted
on the train ride with my father going to Zozzie's house.
But I'd lost her letter. It was back in my purse in Turner's
room. I thought, they'll find it with my money, my name,
everything.

Then Turner said, "I've still got the papers, at least," and
Kate put her hands over her face. "I don't have anything,"
she said.

Traffic was thickening. We were reaching the bridge.
Turner was swinging in and out of lanes, around trucks and
cars, as if trying to put off forever the thing that would happen next. "Stop," Kate said thickly. I couldn't see her face;
perhaps she was crying, perhaps not. "Let's get out and
clean ourselves up. Over there." She pointed with a finger.
"Let's go fix ourselves up or we'll never get across."

Turner obliged. He pulled off the highway and into a lot
that had a gas pump and an adobe hut with a broken door.
We all got out, even the dog, who lifted its leg against the
pump while Turner pulled a piece of money out of his jeans
and went inside with Kate.

Our papers lay on the seat of the car. I was still Turner's
paper wife. But I took Alexander's hand and turned away
and called the dog. Kate could take my place at his side.

I wasn't afraid. Why should I be? This was only land and sky and a dog and a quiet child who held onto me. We began to walk, although my body was sore and the sky hung around us like a caul. There was no sun, no moon, only an ultraviolet light across the folds of land that surrounded us, but I wrapped this drapery around us, as if it were a shield against bitterness.

There was a breeze. It was almost pleasant, like my surprise. I was focussing on my feet, my hands no part of me, my belly gone, but the highway was immense and we moved along its shoulder, a steep roll of gravel and oil, a length of silver as long as the river Kate and Turner had to cross.

I walked along the road wearing a blood-stained cotton dress and sandals. My hair was tied back. I did not want to look unusual, but I was unusual anyway. I had no money, no identity. I was walking with a barefoot, dark-skinned child. Alexander had lost his shoes. He'd left them behind in the rush to get out of the room. But I could feel him holding onto my dress. Otherwise I was outside everything. And I paid attention to the sensation. I was glad to have found it.

I wondered if Kate and Turner would make it to Canada

with their false identities. It was easy, somehow, to imagine Kate there. I saw her walking under trees that were larger, leafier than any she had ever known, trees that provide a different shade, because nothing violent ever happens under them. On warm days, there would be music from an open window, the smell of good food. And someday a child would appear. There would be friends, walls would be lined with books. There would be intense discussions on canvas chairs. Someone getting up. Someone sitting down. Someone changing the record, feeding the cat, giving the child a cup of juice. Laughter.

And Turner would be safe with her.

While Alexander walked beside me, I explained things to him. "Do you know, when I met Kate I was only seven years old. Then one day she took my hand and walked me to her house. We had everything. Think of it." I said. "But it will require very little to live the life ahead of us. A few services to others. A few children to teach. Socorro will bring them," I said, "when we get to her little village. And we'll sit with them outside in the mornings, and it will be possible to look out at our garden, where we will grow everything. We'll collect seeds. And various types of corn. And in the dry years there will be gaps in the kernals, but there will be time for everything."

In this way, while he walked through the hours of that first day, I led Alexander through the years ahead. The sun stayed with us, and the dog, but we had nothing else. "Listen: At the end of October, on the Day of the Dead, we'll put out bread and candles and small sugar skulls for the children. And when the month turns, we'll put out bread and salt and water for your mother and mine.

That evening, we arrived at the entrance of a dusty town where there were women sitting in doorways, with small children playing around them or moving under the folds of their clothes. In front of the church, the smoke of a burning Judas hung in the air. For a long time we stood at the top of the narrow street. We stood like silhouettes, hollow shadows. I took Alexander by the hand and he reached out for the dog and we drifted slowly toward the women and children.

There seemed to be hundreds of women in doorways, hundreds of women as firm as the continent and hundreds of children in the top soil of fabric.

I wondered if I should ask for the market. But it would be closed and we had no money. I should move to them with my head down, I thought, for I am the one in need. "*Lo siento.*" I touched a woman lightly on the sleeve. I was asking if she'd give me some clothes for Alexander because I could see the foot of a child dangling from her lap. But she pulled her dark rebozo back and shook her head and laughed, pointing to a small, round girl on her folded legs and showing me a mouth missing some of its teeth.

Once I would have selected one of these mothers and given my tithe, but that was long ago. Now Alexander pushed his hand out judiciously and one of the women looked at him and held up a large, dark coin. I was tired. I wanted to sit down with these mothers, but Alexander was walking down the line of women in doorways and each of them seemed to be pressing something into his small, bold hand.

"*Por nada,*" one told him sweetly.

"*Qué preciosa,*" another said.

He pointed to me then, to my shoulders and my bare

head. Walking to one of the mothers, he tugged at her shawl, and offered her one of the coins he'd been given. The woman slipped off the long piece of fabric and Alexander awkwardly wrapped it around my arms.

"*Gracias,*" I said bending down in front of him.

Alexander laughed and pointed at his feet. "*Zapatos!*" he reminded me. Then a smile, very sly as I reached for him. Across the street, a jacaranda tree lifted its purple branches. It offered its flowers to the place between earth and sky.